"DO YOU THINK YOU CAN JUST GO AROUND KISSING PEOPLE WITHOUT ANY CONCERN FOR THEIR FEELINGS?"

"You are going to marry my sister," Hannah went on, "and yet you kissed me. You ought not to have done that, you know."

"I am so sorry, Hannah," Miles said. "That was unpardonable of me. It was a mistake. I hope you will forgive me."

"A mistake?" Her voice cracked on the word. "Do you think me such a child that I am immune to your kisses? That I would not understand? That I would not respond? Well, you were wrong, Lord Strickland. I am not a child. I am a woman with a woman's feelings. It was cruel of you to make me feel like that—all warm and soft inside—when you mean to marry my sister and have no interest in me whatsoever. It is not at all what I would expect from a gentleman."

Miles reeled as if struck. "I do not think of you as a child, Hannah. You are a beautiful, intelligent, and desirable woman." As he spoke the words, he suddenly realized how much he meant them. He had not thought of her as a girl when he'd held her in his arms. She had been as responsive and passionate as he might have expected from someone of her uninhibited nature. He smiled with new comprehension. "And I have not asked your sister to marry me," he said.

"I wish to be alone," Hannah said. "Please do not follow me."

Miles smiled at her retreating figure. He saw her with a new clarity, and his heart was full to bursting. He had made a decision.

The Best Intentions

∽∾

Candice Hern

A SIGNET BOOK

SIGNET
Published by New American Library, a division of
Penguin Putnam Inc., 375 Hudson Street,
New York, New York 10014, U.S.A.
Penguin Books Ltd, 27 Wrights Lane,
London W8 5TZ, England
Penguin Books Australia Ltd,
Ringwood, Victoria, Australia
Penguin Books Canada Ltd, 10 Alcorn Avenue,
Toronto, Ontario, Canada M4V 3B2
Penguin Books (N.Z.) Ltd, 182-190 Wairau Road,
Auckland 10, New Zealand

Penguin Books Ltd, Registered Offices:
Harmondsworth, Middlesex, England

First published by Signet, an imprint of New American Library,
a division of Penguin Putnam Inc.

First Printing, June 1999
10 9 8 7 6 5 4 3 2 1

Dedicated to
all my far-flung Berger cousins,
especially Alex,
my biggest fan

Chapter 1

"Whatever fool claimed females to be the weaker sex never met my sister."

Miles Prescott, the Earl of Strickland, slapped the open letter from Lady Tyndall against his palm and heaved an exasperated sigh. He gave the missive one last glance, then, with a derisive snort, neatly refolded it and returned it to the stack of mail on the silver tray placed beside him on the breakfast table. He used his thumb and forefinger to align the corners so the letters sat exactly square upon the tray.

A deep chuckle recalled his attention to his guest, Joseph Wetherby, a close friend and neighbor who had joined him that morning in a brisk ride through the gentle, rolling hills and checkerboard pastures of Northamptonshire.

"And what," Joseph asked, "has the formidable Winifred done now?"

"Nothing yet," Miles replied, "but she is about to." He returned his attention to his breakfast, ravenous after the long ride. "She announces that she and Godfrey and the boys will descend upon Epping in two weeks' time."

"That is not so unusual, is it?" Joseph asked, his fork poised above a slice of beef tongue. "Does she not visit at least once a year? And more often since . . . "

"Indeed," Miles said, finishing his friend's thought,

"she has been a great support to me since Amelia's death."

In fact, Winifred had been a godsend, stepping in to help with Amy and Caro when they most needed a woman's hand, and when he had been paralyzed with grief. She had been a doting aunt to his daughters, especially to Amy, the eldest and most confused by the loss of her mother. For that, Winifred had his eternal gratitude.

Miles was in fact extremely fond of his older sister. Theirs had always been a close family and he never begrudged Winifred a visit to the home where she had grown up. But this time . . .

"This time is different," he said. "This time she is bringing along two of Godfrey's cousins, and her intentions are as transparent as glass. One of the cousins," he said, arching a significant brow, "is a young girl about to make her bow in Society."

"Aha!" Joseph said. "And you think—"

"And I *know*, my friend. I know." He took a roll, still warm from the oven, sliced it into perfect halves, and spread each half evenly from edge to edge with butter. "Winifred does not even attempt to prevaricate," he continued. "She believes it is time I remarried, and nothing will stop her until she has seen me properly settled. And so she is bringing along this young chit for my inspection, along with the girl's older sister, a widow, who is to chaperone her in London next season."

He placed a precise dollop of marmalade in the center of each half roll and spread it carefully so as not to spill over the edges. He laid the knife down across the plate, picked up a half roll between two fingers, and cast his guest an imploring look. "Blast it all, Joseph! A young chit probably just out of the schoolroom."

"Correct me if I'm wrong, Miles," Joseph said, "but had you not decided for yourself that it was time to remarry?" His tone was offhand, his attention firmly fixed on attacking the beef tongue in an almost savage manner that set Miles's teeth on edge.

"Have I not listened to you prattle on and on about how your girls need a mother?" Joseph went on, speaking through bites of beef. "And did you not go down to Chissingworth just last month to begin your search?"

"Yes, yes, of course I did," Miles said with a dismissive wave of his hand. "But I never said as much to Winifred. As if I would! I knew there'd be no stopping her if she got wind of my plans. Granted, I have decided to look for a wife. And granted, I am not very particular about who it is, so long as she gets along with Amy and Caro. But, dammit, I prefer to do my own choosing, if you please." He took two bites of roll, returned it to the plate, and lifted a napkin to touch the corners of his mouth.

"But you just admitted you don't care whom you marry," Joseph said. "Can't say as I approve of such a notion, but that is what you said, ain't it?"

"I did, and I meant it," Miles replied in an irascible tone, "for the most part." He sat back in his chair and mentally shook off the agitation caused by Winifred's letter. There was no need to get upset. He knew his own mind on this matter and had no intention of allowing his redoubtable sister to sway him. This time, he would hold steadfast against her interfering ways. Or so he hoped.

"I'll tell you something, Joe," he said. "I learned a thing or two while at Chissingworth. The one type of woman I want nothing to do with is a young girl in her first Season." He had become quite fixated on this issue. "They may think they want a title and wealth and position. Indeed, their mothers certainly think so. But in the end, it is a love match they want, whether they admit it or not. It's all those romantic books they read, those little purple things. What are they called?"

"Novels."

"I know they're novels, for God's sake. But you know the ones I mean. Those"—he stirred the air with his fingers as he reached for the right words—"those little pasteboard-bound books that flourish at lending libraries. You know the type. Sentimental pap where some aristocratic young fool falls in love with a frightfully ineligible girl—usually a shopkeeper's ward or some such thing—and finally throws sense out the window and swoons in raptures at her feet. Then some dastardly plot is revealed, and she turns out to be the daughter of a duke, and they fall blissfully into each other's arms."

Joseph laughed and Miles gave an ill-tempered snort. "Mawkish, romantical nonsense," he continued. "Almost always written by 'A Lady' or Mrs. So-and-So."

"Or so they claim."

"What?" He looked sharply at his friend. "Do you mean they might actually be written by men? Do you really believe a *man* would be capable of producing such drivel?"

Joseph burst out laughing and Miles had to smile at his own absurdity.

"In any case," he continued when Joseph had seen fit to stop chortling, "those are the sorts of stories young girls are weaned on these days. Not to mention the modern poets and their tedious romanticism."

Thus proving the absurdity of his previous remark about men. Drivel, indeed. Or so he believed, though it was not an opinion he cared to publicize.

"Good Lord," he went on, "the girls' heads are full of the stuff. And so they seek that kind of love for themselves. But I can't offer it to them, Joseph. I can't. I gave all I had to Amelia."

He paused, his chest tightening painfully, as it often did when he thought of his late wife and the cruelly short time they had had together. "She was the one true love of my life." His voice dropped to almost a whisper. "The keeper of my heart."

Miles rose from his chair and approached the sideboard. He was uncomfortable wearing his emotions on his sleeve, or speaking of Amelia in such an intimate manner. But Joseph was almost like family. They had grown up together. Miles could be open with him. To a degree.

He replenished his own and Joseph's coffee, then returned the sterling pot to its place on the sideboard, adjusting its position slightly so the handle was perfectly parallel to the edge of its tray. He absently tightened the lids on several chafing dishes and aligned the handles of all the serving spoons before returning to his seat.

"I cannot expect such good fortune a second time," he continued, feeling more composed. "Nor do I seek it. Amelia will never be replaced in my heart. Our daughters remind me so every day when I look into their little faces. Especially Amy. She looks so like her mother."

He took a deep breath and blew it out through puffed cheeks. "How can I deny a young woman the opportunity for the sort of love I shared with Amelia? It is not fair to her. And I have no wish to live up to those expectations. No, my friend," he said, picking up the other half roll and returning to the matter at hand. "No giddy young miss for me."

"And so, what *are* you looking for?" Joseph asked. "The sadder but wiser girl?"

"Something like that. A woman who has knowledge of love, so I won't feel I am denying her that experience."

"Next time we're in Town I could take you to

Covent Garden," Joseph said. His blue eyes twinkled wickedly as he grinned at Miles. "You will find many such women of experience there."

"You deliberately misunderstand me, Joseph. You are poking fun at me when I am quite serious. I tell you I have had my fill of young women who believe they want nothing more than my rank and fortune when they in fact are seeking much more."

"You discovered all this during one month at Chissingworth?"

"Indeed." Joseph gave him an inquiring look, but Miles had no desire to discuss his rebuffed proposal to Miss Forsythe. Though the whole episode had turned out well—he was sincerely pleased that his friend Stephen had found such happiness—it was nevertheless a sobering experience.

In the first place, it had never occurred to him that any woman would actually refuse him. He was an earl with a large fortune and, though he had always thought of himself as perfectly ordinary, he knew women found him attractive. He was given to understand that he had everything a young woman could ask for. With an arrogance that shamed him in retrospect, he had not even considered the possibility of a refusal.

In the second place, when it became clear that the young woman was in love with someone else and had only encouraged Miles's attentions because his rank and fortune were thought to be superior, he realized he had seriously miscalculated. It had been a near miss. If the young woman had not followed her heart in the end, he might have been saddled with a wife miserable with love for someone else. And all because he had been looking for the wrong sort of woman—the typical young miss ready to enter the Marriage Mart.

Exactly the sort of young woman his sister was bringing to Epping in two weeks' time.

"And so," Joseph said, "tell me again about this sadder but wiser girl you're not very particular about." He took a third helping of tongue as Miles watched in fascination. How the fellow could pack away so much food and still remain thin was a puzzle he'd never solved. But then, it *had* been quite a vigorous ride.

"An older woman, to be sure," Miles said at last. "No schoolroom misses for me." He actually shuddered at the thought. "Someone who is primarily looking for security and comfort, with no expectations of love. Someone who could be happy living quietly here in the country with my girls and . . . and with me."

"A widow, perhaps?"

"Perhaps." In deference to his own appetite, Miles began carefully tapping at the shell of a boiled egg, perched in a delicate Worcester eggcup. "Yes," he said. "Yes, a widow would do quite nicely."

"And did you not say that Winifred is also bringing along the chit's sister, a widow?"

"By Jove, she did say that," he said as he neatly lifted off in one piece the precisely split top of the eggshell. "Here, let me see . . . " He put aside his spoon, took up the letter once again, and scanned it until he found the relevant passage. "She is Godfrey's widowed cousin, a Lady Abingdon." He looked up at his friend. "Have you any knowledge of a Lady Abingdon, Joe?"

"Abingdon. Hmm. Sounds vaguely familiar. It is possible I met her at the Carruthers' ball last season. Could she have a connection to him as well?"

"I've no idea. What was she like?"

Joseph smiled, leaned back in his chair, and clasped his hands behind his head. "Let me see. Fortyish. Sharp-featured. Rail thin. She wore dark purple, as I recall. And plumes. Lots of plumes."

Miles stifled a gasp.

"But perhaps that was Lady Atherton, not Abingdon." Joseph flashed a grin. "I could be mistaken."

"Good God, I hope so."

"Aha, then you *are* somewhat particular after all."

"Well," Miles said, casting a sheepish look at his grinning friend, "I suppose I am at that." He put aside the letter and with the tiny silver spoon began to scoop out the boiled egg from its shell. "I should prefer her to be young enough to . . . well, I would rather like more children, I believe. A son, you know. An heir."

"Then perhaps you had better stick with the young chit," Joseph said. "Leave the widow to me."

"To you?"

"A lonely widow, stuck in the Shires weeks before hunting season, forced to haul around her young charge. The poor woman may be bored to death. It is possible I can offer her some . . . diversion during her stay."

"Dalliance, you mean."

"Whatever happens, happens." Joseph ran his fingers absently through his thinning blond hair and smiled rakishly. "Besides," he said, "if Winifred is bringing two women, you will have odd numbers. You need an extra man, and I am happy to be at your service, my lord."

"Good heavens," Miles said, looking up from his egg. "You are right. Of course you must join us. And if the widow is as you described, you are welcome to her. If, on the other hand, she is younger and reasonably handsome—"

"Then you shall have first crack at her."

"Good Lord! You make it sound positively sordid. I am not looking for a mistress. I am looking for a wife."

"And I, happily, am not."

"Well, just in case the widow is not quite what you recollect," Miles continued, "I should like a chance to become acquainted, to pursue a respectable friendship, at least."

"You shall have first right of refusal, mine host," Joseph said, helping himself to a thick slice of bread. "But truly, Miles, Lady Abingdon is probably not at all the same woman I am thinking of. It is unlikely she would be in her forties with a younger sister just out of the schoolroom."

"But Winifred says the chit—I beg your pardon, her name is Hannah, Miss Hannah Fairbanks—is only a half sister to Lady Abingdon. They had the same father. His second marriage might have been decades after his first. There could well be a gulf of twenty years or more between the sisters."

"Hmm. We shall just have to wait and see. But I will act as your silent watchdog, Miles, to protect you against unwanted advances from whichever of the two women you decide you do not want."

"You would be put to better use protecting me against Winifred," Miles said, "to see that she doesn't push me into something I do not want."

"Do not worry about Winifred," Joseph said. "I have known her all these years and I assure you I am not the least bit afraid of her."

"You should be. What if she decides to set her mind on finding a wife for *you*?"

"Good God!"

"We had better bring along this one, too."

Hannah Fairbanks peered over the rim of her book to see her sister, Charlotte, Lady Abingdon, hold up a delicate blue satin evening dress for inspection. Bored to the bone with all the fuss and bother, Hannah watched with supreme indifference as her sister gently shook out the net overdress, checked the satin *rouleau* and rich blond lace of the deep flounce, and nodded her approval before handing the dress over to the maid standing at her side.

"Take all these, Lily," Charlotte said to the maid, "and prepare them for packing."

Hannah chewed on her lower lip to keep from giggling as poor little Lily, her arms overladen with an enormous pile of dresses, bobbed an awkward curtsey and backed unsteadily out of the bedchamber.

"What a pack of nonsense, Lottie," Hannah said, and then leaned back against the bed pillows and propped the book open upon her knees. "I cannot possibly need all those clothes at Epping Hall. And especially not that silly little ball dress you insisted on having made. It is not the Season yet, you know. I still have hopes of discovering some emergency to keep me away from *that* nightmare for another year. In the meantime," she said, flipping through the pages of *Ancient Castles of England and Wales*, "I plan to enjoy this respite in Northamptonshire by tramping about the countryside and examining the local architecture. Do you know some of the finest examples of both Saxon and Norman architecture can be found within a very short distance from Epping Hall? Not to mention the ruins of—"

"I will not have you roaming about in muddied hems at every opportunity," Charlotte interrupted in that imperious tone she had honed to a fine edge, the tone that told Hannah it was useless to argue. She had long ago learned to nod deferentially, like a dutiful younger sister, and then go ahead and do precisely as she pleased. Though she was coming to believe that such would not be the case this time. For reasons quite unfathomable to Hannah, her sister seemed determined to fire her off next Season, to get her up as a real lady and foist her off onto some unsuspecting gentleman. Absurd!

"Now put your knees down, sit up straight, and listen to me!" Charlotte snapped.

Hannah heaved a dramatic sigh. She closed her book, swung her legs over the side of the bed and sat up ramrod straight. "I'm listening," she said, though she was doing no such thing. Her stocking-clad feet bounced against the bed boards as she thought longingly of the opportunity to explore the Saxon Church of St. Biddulph in the village of Eppingham.

"Epping Hall," Charlotte went on, "is the seat of an earl. It is a fine and elegant country home. There are sure to be other guests, though Winifred insists on referring to it as an intimate family gathering. We shall make the best of this opportunity to prepare you for the Season in Town."

Hannah groaned.

"While with the earl's family," Charlotte continued, "you will learn to behave like a lady. You will not speak in stable cant, nor will you ramble on in that bookish manner of yours. And," she said with a steely glint in her gray eyes, "you will remember to think before you speak. I will not have you embarrassing us all with one of your ill-timed, outrageous outbursts. And as for that lovely ball dress, I can assure you that you will indeed need it. Cousin Winifred tells me that the annual threshing ball will be held at Epping Hall during our stay."

Hannah gave a snort of laughter. "A threshing ball? How elegant. Are you sure the blue satin dress is fine enough? Perhaps I could attach a corn doll to the bodice."

Charlotte rolled her eyes heavenward. "Hannah, my girl, where is your brain? Despite the seemingly bucolic occasion, I can assure you that *any* ball given at Epping Hall will be a dignified and stately affair. It will be the perfect opportunity to ease you into Society before taking you to London in the spring. And I expect you to make a good impression, not just at the ball but at all times during our stay. You will practice genteel, demure conversation at all times—"

"Rules!" Hannah interrupted. "You and your endless rules."

"My dear child, civilized Society is governed by rules. It is time you grew up and learned to live with them."

"You are determined to break me, Lottie, are you not? Like some unmanageable colt."

"My dear," Charlotte said, her voice softening, "I am only trying to help. It is time and past that you made your bow to Society. You must learn to behave like the well-bred young lady you are. It is not so much a matter of rules. It is more a question of common courtesy."

Hannah shrank back as though she'd been slapped. Her cheeks flamed with embarrassment. Was she really so backward? So uncouth?

"And so," Charlotte went on, "you must try to curb your tongue. You do say the most shocking things at times, you know. We will make certain that you have a suitable wardrobe as well. A wardrobe fitting for a young lady. You will dress properly during the days as well as the evenings. You will— Oh, good heavens. What about shoes?"

Charlotte turned to the tall mahogany wardrobe and began rummaging about the upper shelves. "Oh, Hannah!" she wailed. "Look at these!" She held up a pair of comfortable yellow kid half boots, scuffed and dirty from a recent encounter with a mud puddle— Hannah had not been paying attention to where she was walking. "And these." Charlotte then held up an old pair of pink silk slippers that had seen better days. The fabric had split and the toes were dark with something. Hannah couldn't recall when she'd worn them last. "Oh, Hannah. Do you have even a single pair of decent shoes?"

Hannah shrugged, wondering what was wrong with the kid boots. "I have lived in the country all my life, Lottie. Silk slippers are not exactly conducive to country lanes and gravel paths."

"Do you have nothing that is not worn outdoors?" Charlotte asked as she returned the offensive shoes to the wardrobe shelf.

Hannah looked down at her stocking-clad feet and wiggled her toes. "I never thought about it much, I suppose," she said. "I don't pay much attention to what shoes I wear, so long as they are comfortable."

"Hannah." Charlotte pressed her fingers to her temples and groaned. "You are a sore trial to me, my girl. You are not even trying to help."

Hannah watched her sister's obvious distress and felt a niggling twinge of self-reproach. Perhaps she *was* being childish. She really didn't mean to get Lottie's hackles up. She never deliberately set out to do that. It just always seemed to happen somehow. But all this fuss about dressing Hannah up like a lady had all the signs of a monumental waste of time. She would never be the beautiful, elegant, sophisticated woman her sister was.

Well, perhaps it wouldn't hurt to play along with Charlotte for once. She meant well, after all.

"Wait a moment," Hannah said as she jumped down from the bed and walked to the wardrobe. "I have these." She pulled down a box from the top shelf, opened it, removed the silver tissue, and pulled out a pristine pair of blue satin slippers. "Remember? You had these made to match the blue evening dress."

"Oh, yes! Of course. Thank heavens." Charlotte fingered the blue satin with a satisfied sigh. "Well," she said, wrapping them back up in their protective tissue, "let us at least try to keep them in good condition until we arrive at Epping Hall."

"I promise not to wear them until then," Hannah said.

Charlotte put the box on a table near the bedchamber door, obviously ready to hand them over to Lily for packing. She would not trust Hannah to remember her promise. Hannah blanched at the implication, but let it pass. She didn't even like the slippers anyway.

"We'll go into Dudley tomorrow and see about more shoes for you," Charlotte said. "But you must promise not to tramp all about Epping with them in the mud."

Hannah was not about to make that promise. There was St. Biddulph's, after all.

"Why is this so important to you, Lottie?" she asked. "Why are you so determined to turn me into a fine lady? You know it will never work. I'll never take."

"Oh, but of course you will, my dear. If you will only make an effort."

"But why?"

"I want you to make a good impression at Epping Hall," Charlotte said.

"On whom, may I ask? Oh. Oh, no. Do not tell me there will be some young man there you've already picked out for me? Lottie!"

"I do not know whom we might meet at Epping Hall," Charlotte said. "I merely want you to make a good impression on the earl."

"Why? Because he is cousin Godfrey's brother-in-law?"

"There is that, of course. Such connections should be honored. But he is . . . he is a widower, you know."

"A widower?" Hannah conjured an image of a plump, balding, middle-aged gentleman in search of a new wife. Is this what her sister had in mind for her? "Oh, no, Lottie. No. Surely you do not expect me to—"

"No, of course not," Charlotte said with an impatient wave of her hand. "You are much too young."

"I should think so," Hannah muttered. And suddenly, understanding dawned upon her. Charlotte was still a young woman, not quite thirty, and had been widowed just over two years. She was not the sort of woman who could live comfortably without a man. "Oho! Now I see!" Hannah said with a triumphant wave of her hand. "A widower indeed. A rich one, too, no doubt—with a fine, elegant country estate. You want him for yourself!"

"Hannah—"

"You think perhaps this widowed earl will make a good second husband for you, do you not?" Hannah watched her sister's pained expression and knew it was more than just that. "And you don't want your gauche little sister to spoil your chances."

Charlotte looked down at her hands and did not reply. Good heavens, Hannah had hit the mark. She was an embarrassment to her sister. Charlotte wanted to seriously pursue this fine lord without the added baggage of an unmarried, bookish bumpkin under her wing—an unwanted relation the earl might have to take in if he married Charlotte. And so Hannah was to be transformed into a lady and married off as quickly as possible.

Well, she had no intention of marrying, regardless of her sister's machinations. Courtship and marriage had never interested her, though at nineteen it should have been uppermost in her mind, she supposed. But Hannah had never harbored foolish romantical notions, and she had no maternal instincts that she was aware of. The only true pleasures in her life were her books and her architectural studies. She did not wish to marry.

And she would not allow Charlotte to force her into something she did not want. Of course, as an unmarried young woman she was obliged to depend upon others. Since her mother's death last year, she had been dependent upon Charlotte. She would prefer to live alone with her books, but she knew it was not allowed. Charlotte would certainly not allow it. But Charlotte need not feel responsible for Hannah. She had a brother, after all. A half brother, really, Charlotte's brother. Bertram had never much liked her, but his wife was very friendly and would certainly welcome Hannah into their household, if necessary.

Hannah would keep this strategy to herself for the time being. Charlotte had this bee in her bonnet about firing off Hannah into Society and would not be stopped. Hannah would play along as best she could, but in the end, she would go to Bertram. Charlotte could have her earl.

"It is true," Charlotte said at last, "that I have considered the idea of the earl as a possible suitor. Winifred speaks so highly of him, she has me quite intrigued." She caught Hannah's eye and grinned sheepishly, ignoring her sister's last comment and the awkward silence that had followed. "She tells me he is quite handsome."

Hannah saw the twinkle in her sister's eye and laughed. Charlotte loved her, after all, and despite her muddleheaded notions of turning Hannah out as a lady, she meant well. And so why shouldn't she have her handsome earl? "And I have no doubt," Hannah said, "that Winifred has told him how beautiful you are. He will fall in love with you on first sight and write odes to your auburn hair and sonnets praising the perfect swell of your white bosom."

"Really, Hannah!"

"And you will be a countess. No wonder that you wish me to become a lady. After all, I am to be the sister of a countess!"

"My dear," Charlotte said with a smile, "you are

putting the cart before the horse. Perhaps he is an ogre. Perhaps he will not take a liking to me."

Hannah laughed. "But of course he will." Which was nothing but the truth. If anyone knew how to encourage the attentions of a gentleman, it was Charlotte. She had let nothing stop her in her pursuit of Sir Lionel Abingdon some years back. If she wanted this earl, no doubt she would have him.

Hannah wished her joy of the chase and hoped she would be thoroughly diverted while at Epping Hall. For while Charlotte was occupied with the earl, Hannah intended to be occupied with St. Biddulph's.

Chapter 2

"Really, Hannah. Must you sit with your nose pressed to the window in that childish manner? You will have Cousin Winifred thinking you a bumpkin who has never before been more than two miles from home."

Hannah ignored her sister and continued to stare at the view with barely suppressed excitement. She was determined to get a good look at this unfamiliar countryside, with its tantalizing landscape of church spires, before they lost the sun.

"I have never before visited Northamptonshire," Hannah said without turning from her view out the window. She sighed wistfully at the thought of tramping from one village to the next, making a close study of the development of early medieval architecture in this part of England. "It is quite, quite wonderful," she muttered softly, her breath clouding the carriage window. She wiped the glass with the sleeve of her pelisse and heard her sister's exasperated groan.

This irritating and all too frequent sound was tempered by the gentle laugh of Winifred, Lady Tyndall, who sat facing Hannah on the opposite bench. "Good heavens, child," she said, "what can you possibly find so interesting in the endless flat fields and criss-crossed hedgerows? I own I am pleased you find the countryside of my childhood to your liking. But I confess it has always seemed rather homely and undistinguished to me. Especially since leaving it."

"Oh, but it is quite distinguished, indeed, Cousin Winifred," Hannah replied. "Only look at all the sturdy church towers and elegant broach spires. This area is ever so rich in early church architecture, as you must know. There were very few examples of Saxon or Norman buildings in our part of Shropshire. Truly, I feel like a child at Christmas."

"As I am sure Cousin Winifred has noticed," Charlotte said in the perturbed tone she had been using with increasing frequency since leaving Dudley-on-the-Meese. "The way you positively shrieked as we passed through Earls Barton, determined that we must all stop and visit that hideous tower thing. It really is too much, Hannah. I should never have allowed Winifred and Godfrey to indulge you in such foolishness."

At that, Hannah felt compelled to pull her gaze from the passing scenery and glare openmouthed at Charlotte. "That *hideous tower thing*," she said, stunned that her own sister could be so frightfully ignorant, "is a tenth-century Saxon church tower, for God's sake."

"Hannah!" Charlotte snapped. "Watch your language, young lady."

"Sorry," Hannah said. "But when was the last time you saw a Saxon tower?"

"I am sure I do not know," Charlotte replied. "And if they are all as ugly as that one, I am sure I never hope to see another."

Hannah snorted in disbelief and turned back to watch the view. She marveled at people like Charlotte who could not see beyond the surface of things, who only found beauty in buildings trimmed in gilt and geegaw. But now was not the time to consider her sister's want of understanding. They should be nearing Eppingham very soon—and St. Biddulph's, the church she longed to see more than anything else.

"What I *do* care about," Charlotte continued, "is seeing Epping Hall at last. The Jewel of the Shires."

Cousin Winifred chuckled. "I am sure I am quite prejudiced," she said, "but I have always believed that sobriquet to be no less than it deserves. We are all very proud of Epping. And Hannah, my dear, though I know it is not medieval—and therefore unworthy of serious consideration—I think you might find it interesting nonetheless." She laughed again. "There are a few remaining bits of the old Tudor hall, but the primary design was provided almost two hundred years ago by Inigo Jones."

"Yes," Hannah replied in a distracted manner. "I recall reading about it." A tiny cough from Charlotte reminded Hannah of her promise to be polite and genteel. She turned toward Winifred and smiled. "I am sure it is exceedingly beautiful," she said. In fact, the prints she had seen of Epping Hall, especially those of its interiors, did not appeal to her in the least. Too fussy and baroque by half. But it was an important house, to be sure. She would put aside her personal opinions and see what she could learn of England's great architect.

"I look forward to seeing the house," she said, more sincerely this time, "and studying Mr. Jones's designs up close."

"You must ask my brother, the earl, to show you about, my dear," Winifred said. "He knows the old place better than anyone and loves to show it off. And he loves to boast that Epping has passed directly from father to son, in unbroken descent from the first earl, who was granted the land by King Henry VIII."

"Indeed?" Charlotte said. "No cousins or brothers or uncles have ever inherited?"

"Not a one," Winifred said. "Each countess was clever enough to present her lord with a healthy heir.

Miles is the eleventh earl, you know. And his first wife, poor thing, died before she could do her duty."

Hannah tightened her hold on the strap and stifled the urge to deliver a scathing retort. *Do her duty*, indeed. It was enough to make a person ill. Yet without even looking, she could sense her sister's piqued interest. She could feel her shift her position, to straighten slightly on the bench.

God's teeth! Was the beautiful, elegant Charlotte going to allow herself to be made into a brood mare for this wretched earl, just so he could continue the unbroken line of Stricklands?

"It was the fourth earl," Winifred went on in a casual tone as though she had not just uttered such absolute nonsense, "who had most of the old Tudor hall demolished and built the current manor house. But each Earl of Strickland has made his seat at an estate on the same spot for over three hundred years."

"How lovely to have such an enduring legacy," Charlotte said in her most engaging tone. Hannah suspected she was already imagining her own role in ensuring the unbroken lineage of such a noble house. What a pity if Cousin Winifred had exaggerated and the earl turned out to be a fat, foul-smelling lout of a man with most of his teeth missing. But Charlotte would no doubt overlook such trivialities in order to *do her duty*.

"To have such firmly planted ancestral roots in one place is really quite awe-inspiring," Charlotte went on, pressing the point more than Hannah thought absolutely necessary. "You quite intrigue me, Winifred. I am tempted to call out to the coachman to make haste so that we may see Epping Hall at last. Indeed, I—"

"Oh. Oh. *Oh!*" Hannah almost knocked her head against the coach ceiling as she bounced with sudden excitement. "I see it! I see it! There it is!"

Winifred turned in her seat and craned her neck

around to look out the opposite window. "Can you see it already?" she asked. "Oh, yes. Yes. there it is. You can just see the Old Tower peeking above the trees. Over there, Charlotte. Do you see?"

"Is it not wonderful?" Hannah exclaimed. "Is it not fabulous? Is it not the most incredibly beautiful thing you have ever seen?"

"I can only just make out a small cupola and finial, I believe," Charlotte said in a puzzled tone. "But I am sure as soon as we move beyond the trees and across the river to get a clear view, I will certainly find it the most beautiful thing I have ever seen."

"Hannah, my dear child," said Winifred, "what on earth are you looking at? You cannot see Epping Hall from that window."

"I would not know about that," Hannah replied, nose pressed firmly to the glass. "But I can see St. Biddulph's, and it is a most wondrous sight indeed."

Miles stood on the steps of the Tudor porch in the inner courtyard and watched his brother-in-law's elegant carriage make its way through the open archway. Godfrey himself rode close behind on horseback. It was like him, Miles thought, to steer clear of a carriage full of females. Another carriage could be seen coming up the straight gravel path from the gatehouse. Winifred's luggage, no doubt. With two additional ladies along, Miles wondered how many other carriages poor Godfrey had been forced to bring. But there was no time to find out as the first carriage rolled to a halt at the porch steps.

Miles kept his hands clasped tightly behind his back. He experienced an unexpected twinge of nervousness at the prospect of meeting the young woman who had almost certainly been brought to Epping Hall for consideration as his future countess. Though he had every intention of remaining steadfast in his refusal to be a party to his sister's infernal matchmaking and trust to his own inclinations in the matter, he nevertheless harbored a nagging curiosity about the young woman. Had she been encouraged to expect a formal courtship from him? Perhaps even an offer?

The devil take Winifred and her confounded interference.

A footman put down the steps and opened the carriage door. Miles offered a hand to Winifred, who gave him a broad smile as she emerged from the carriage.

"Winifred, my dear, it is good to see you," he said, keeping hold of her hand. Despite his trepidation about this visit, he meant it. He was always glad to see her. "You look wonderful. One would hardly guess you have been traveling for days."

"Your flattery is wasted on me, Miles," she said and offered her cheek for his kiss. "But I have brought along two ladies who may have more appreciation for it." She tilted her head toward the open carriage door.

Miles narrowed his brows in a quick scowl for her eyes only, then turned to hand out the first of the other passengers. His proffered hand was taken by the nearest of the two ladies, who ducked beneath the door and stepped out in a single fluid movement. She was slender and wore a dark green pelisse and matching bonnet. Although he knew little about such things, he felt certain the bonnet, with its brim turned up at the front and a small ostrich feather sweeping down over it, would be considered the height of fashion. Winifred spoke before Miles had time to steady the woman and release her hand.

"Miles, allow me to present to you Godfrey's cousin, Lady Abingdon. Charlotte, my dear, this is my brother, Lord Strickland."

So, this was the chaperone, Miles thought as he released her hand. She looked up at him for the first time briefly before dropping into a curtsey, and it was only due to years—nay, generations—of good breeding that his composure did not slip. This was no pinch-faced, aging duenna. Though clearly not in the first bloom of youth, she was strikingly pretty. Soft auburn curls arranged themselves artfully along the bonnet's upturned brim, and its plume curved against a fair-skinned cheek that could not belong to the fortyish widow Joseph had described. This was a young and beautiful woman.

Collecting himself before he began to gape like a schoolboy, Miles nodded in acknowledgment of her curtsey. "Welcome to Epping Hall, Lady Abingdon," he said. "I hope you will enjoy your stay here."

"It is a pleasure to meet you at last, my lord," she said in a voice so soft, it was little more than a whisper, and Miles had to lean forward in order to catch every word. Her gray eyes drew him closer and twinkled with something that eradicated the initial impression of youth and innocence. All at once she was the sophisticated widow, and Joseph's notion of a bit of dalliance seemed not so far-fetched after all. Damn the man for putting such an idea in his head.

"Cousin Winifred has spoken often of you and of Epping Hall," she went on in that maddeningly soft voice, her eyes never leaving his. "My sister and I cannot thank you enough for allowing us to visit."

Ah, yes. The sister. Her charge. "You are both most welcome," Miles said as he reluctantly turned his attention back to the carriage. The figure inside was busily gathering up what looked to be books and papers strewn about the floor at her feet. "Miss Fairbanks, I believe?" He held out a hand to help her down the steps.

She looked up, but, still enveloped in shadows, Miles could not make out her features. "Oh. Thanks, awfully," she said and thrust a stack of books toward him.

He only just managed to grab them in time before she let go, and the unexpected and unwieldy pile bobbled precariously in his hands for an instant before he was able to get a good grip. The tiniest of gasps, apparently emanating from Lady Abingdon, was followed by the familiar sound of his sister's chuckle.

Curse it all, what was going on here?

Miles lifted a brow and a footman was instantly at his side, retrieving the books and patiently awaiting any other items that might precede the exit of the young lady. In fact, only one more untidy stack of papers and notebooks was forthcoming, this one with a pen box and a small pair of compasses perched on top. The footman took them and stood aside.

Once again, Miles reached out a hand, somewhat more tentatively this time. "Miss Fairbanks?"

A small gloved hand took his. As he gently guided the young woman out of the carriage, he noticed dark smudges on the fingertips of her gloves. Despite his gentle efforts, the girl practically tumbled down the steps. One hand held onto a lopsided straw bonnet, attempting to straighten it as she descended. Her efforts were for naught. The bonnet listed slightly to the left and its bow of wide blue ribbon hung limply beneath her chin.

Miles kept hold of her hand to steady her. She looked up at him with huge, guileless blue eyes. "Oh, dear," she said. "Are you the earl?"

Miles was quite simply dumbstruck. The girl standing before him could not be a day above sixteen. A mass of unruly brown curls spilled out from beneath the skewed bonnet. A sprinkling of freckles danced across a pert nose. But the small, heart-shaped face—very similar though slightly more rounded than that of her sister—was dominated by the enormous blue eyes that stared up at him, awaiting his response.

Good Lord, she was only a child. What could Winifred be thinking, expecting him to pay court to this . . . this schoolgirl?

He quickly composed himself and determined not to let his sister out of his sight before having a serious discussion with her.

"Yes, I am afraid I am indeed the earl," he said and offered a smile to the girl, hoping to put her more at ease.

"Miles," Winifred said, "allow me to present to you Miss Fairbanks, Lady Abingdon's sister. Hannah, my dear, meet my brother, Lord Strickland."

"I am pleased to make your acquaintance, Miss Fairbanks," he said. "Welcome to Epping."

"My lord," the girl said and bobbed a creditable curtsey.

What she did next almost knocked him off his pins. While looking him straight in the eye, a huge grin spread across her face, forming two deep dimples in her cheeks. Then she glanced over to her sister, raised her brows, and cocked her head toward him. "Not bad, Lottie," she said.

Good God.

Another tiny gasp came from the direction of Lady Abingdon.

So, the girl had indeed been apprised of a potential match between them and found herself pleased with the situation.

Winifred chuckled again, and he would like to have throttled her on the spot.

"Oh, dear," Miss Fairbanks muttered. "I'm in for it now, aren't I?" She cast an earnest look at Miles, who was busily planning ways to murder his sister. "I do beg your pardon, my lord. Things just seem to pop out of my mouth before I know it. But you see, we had thought . . . well, you being an earl and all and already having a family . . . we thought . . . that is, I thought . . . well, I thought you would be older and not so . . . not so . . . I thought you would be different, you see. Well, of course Cousin Winifred told Lottie you were handsome, but she's your sister, isn't she, so she would have to say that. And so, we didn't know what you'd be like, did we?"

Miles had no idea how to respond to such a speech. Winifred, however, burst into laughter. What sort of joke was his sister playing? "Hannah, my dear child," she said, "you ought to have listened to me. Though I am loathe to admit it publicly, there is no getting around the fact that Miles is my *younger* brother, don't you know."

"Oh." Miss Fairbanks smiled again and the dimples reappeared as she returned her attention to Miles. "Well, I am pleased to meet you, my lord. I am truly sorry for having conjured up such unflattering images of you. And I hope that you will not hold it against Lott—"

"I believe you have said quite enough, Hannah," Lady Abingdon said, her voice as soft as before but decidedly firm.

At that moment, Godfrey, bless the man, joined the group and brought an end to this awkward conversation.

"Hullo, Miles," he said and gave his brother-in-law a hearty slap on the back. "How d'you do, old man? How d'you do? Good to see you. Ah, here're the boys."

A third carriage had pulled up, and almost before it came to a full stop, the door was flung open and two small, freckled-faced boys bounded out and ran to their father.

"Slow down, you little wags. Slow down," Godfrey

said with a fond smile at his sons. "Come say hello to your uncle Miles. Say hello."

Miles crouched down and beckoned the boys to him. The twins threw themselves against him with their usual exuberance, almost knocking him over. His dignity was no match for youth and enthusiasm. "Hold on, lads," he said, "don't throw me to the ground just yet, if you please. Not in front of the ladies."

"Oh, they won't mind," said young Henry as Miles ruffled his hair. " 'Specially not Hannah. She's a right one, she is."

"Is she now, Charlie?"

"I'm *not* Charlie," the boy said with a gap-toothed grin, anticipating the who's who game they always played with their doting uncle.

"You're not?"

"No, *I'm* Charlie," the other boy announced.

"So you are," Miles said, ruffling Charlie's tousled hair. "Then you must be Henry," he said to the first boy. "When will I ever learn to tell one from the other? I have it." He reached a hand into his coat pocket. "I shall simply have to draw a large H on your forehead and a large C on yours. Shall I?"

"No, no, no," the boys shrieked and squirmed as Miles pulled a piece of charcoal from his pocket, put there in anticipation of their arrival, and teased them with it.

"Enough, you little demons," Winifred said, pulling the eight-year-olds away from Miles's threatening charcoal. "And you are just as bad, Miles, tormenting them like that. How shall I ever teach them manners with you and Godfrey as models?"

Miles arched a brow at Winifred, and she grinned. They both knew that no one was more conscious of manners and propriety than the Earl of Strickland.

"Miss Barton," Winifred said, waving toward the

prim governess, who stood quietly beside the carriage looking the worse for wear. But who wouldn't, after three days confined in a carriage with two rambunctious boys? "Take them away and beat them soundly until they learn to behave like gentlemen," his sister continued. "You know the way to the nursery."

"Yes, my lady," the governess said. After both boys had been hugged and kissed by their mother, giving lie to her harsh words, Miss Barton took them each by the hand and followed a footman into the hall.

"Come up later, Hannah?" one of the twins shouted as he was being led away.

"Try and stop me, Charlie," the girl replied.

"I believe we should all be seeking our rooms," Winifred said. "It has been a long trip."

"Indeed," Miles said. "Mrs. Harvey?"

The housekeeper, who had been standing regally in the doorway, quietly directing Epping footmen, visiting maids, and baggage into the hall, now stepped forward. "Yes, my lord." Nodding to Winifred and the other ladies, she said, "This way, if you please," and led the way into the vestibule, through the Great Hall and up the Grand Staircase.

Miles put a restraining hand on his sister's arm as she approached the stairs. "A word with you please, Winifred."

She turned around and glared at him. "Now?"

"Now."

She heaved a weary sigh. "All right," she said, "but let us be quick about it. I am anxious to be out of these traveling clothes and am in great need of a restorative cup of tea."

He led her to a corner of the Great Hall where a grouping of carved oak chairs from the seventeenth century stood against a wall. He indicated that she should be seated.

"Good heavens, Miles," she said after settling her-

self comfortably, "what on earth have I done to bring
on that murderous look of yours?"

"You know very well what you have done."

"I am sure I do not. Have we come at an inconve-
nient time? If so, you had but to tell me, my dear, and
we would have postponed the trip. But you know
Godfrey. He would steal a march on the masses that
will gather in November for the hunts. He will shoot
all your grouse if you don't keep a close watch on
him."

"That is not the issue, and you know it," Miles said.

Winifred sank back against the chair. "It is his
cousins, is it not? You would not have had me bring
them."

"I would not have you managing my life for me."

"Oh, bother," she said with a dismissive wave of
her hand. "I am not trying to manage anything. It is
just that it is high time you thought of marrying
again—"

"Winifred—"

"—and I know you will not make any sort of effort
on your own behalf."

"Hmph," he snorted. He was not about to tell her of
his abortive efforts on his own behalf last month at
Chissingworth.

"I merely brought along a perfectly lovely lady who
might, just might, make you a suitable countess. But I
am not 'managing' anything. It is up to you to—"

"Winifred!" Miles's voice rose with irritation.
"She's just a child!"

"What?"

"How can you imagine," he said in an exasperated
tone, "that I would even entertain the idea of courting
a girl who cannot be much above sixteen years old?"

Winifred glared at him. "Miles, you idiot."

"I am sorry, Winifred, but I will not—"

"My dear brother, I am not so stupid as you seem to

think, though I must tell you that Hannah is in fact older than she looks. She is nineteen, Miles, soon to be twenty."

He raised his brows in disbelief. "Even so—"

"And poor Charlotte despairs of ever properly firing the girl off," Winifred continued. "She has no polish, as you no doubt observed, and fights every attempt to be made into a lady. I will say, though, that she does clean up rather nicely. Hannah can look quite lovely when she makes an effort."

"Yes, but I will not be the one to—"

"It is just that making the effort doesn't seem to be important to her. Her thoughts are always elsewhere. Thinks of nothing but her old buildings and churches and such. So many stops we had to make along the way! Including that perfectly horrid old tower at Earls Barton. The poor thing has had so few opportunities to be out and about, what with her mother's illness and death and then the year's mourning, that I felt obliged to indulge her a bit. Oh, and I did promise, by the by, that you would show her around the hall. She is quite a keen student of architecture, my dear. Though she is devoted to all things Saxon, I suspect you could pique her interest in Epping. She seemed anxious to hear all about Mr. Jones."

"Yes, of course," Miles said impatiently. "But really, Winifred, she is so young. You cannot truly believe I would have the least interest in courting the girl."

"No, of course not, you ninny. I haven't a clue what is to be done about Hannah. I brought Charlotte for you."

"Charlotte?"

"Yes," Winifred replied, with a look that clearly said she thought him a complete fool. "Lady Abingdon. Surely you noticed her? She's a widow these last two years and more, and has no children of her own, poor dear. But then, Lord Abingdon was quite a bit older. Charlotte's not quite thirty, and she's very beautiful. Silly me, I thought you might suit."

Lady Abingdon? Not the scruffy schoolgirl with the uncontrollable tongue, but the lovely widow of the soft voice and sultry eyes? Winifred thought they might suit, did she?

"Indeed, my dear," he said, "you intrigue me."

"Aha! The beautiful widow intrigues you."

Miles hesitated, pacing in front of Winifred's chair. He had, after all, decided that if he married again, he wanted a more mature woman. Could the stunning Lady Abingdon be the right woman? Would she be able to accept him on his own terms? Would she like his daughters? Would they like her? Could she be content with a home, security, and no more than a general sort of affection? Would she understand that he could not offer love or passion?

Hold on a moment, he thought, and stopped pacing. She was a beautiful woman. And she had given him a look that spoke volumes, or so he believed. Perhaps he was being too hasty—about the passion, anyway.

He turned to face his sister. "Yes," he said. "I am intrigued."

Winifred gave a shriek worthy of her sons, flew out of her chair and threw her arms around her brother. "This is an historic moment, my dear," she said. "A day for the annals of Prescott history!"

"Hold on, madam. As always, you jump to conclusions. I said I was intrigued, not that I would marry the woman."

"Oh, that is neither here nor there," she said, "and entirely up to you in any case. The really important thing is that this is the first time in memory you have agreed with me on anything of significance."

"Is it?"

"It is."

"Well then," he said with a mock scowl, "I should hate to ruin an unbroken record of contrariness. Perhaps I should rethink the entire matter." His scowl became a teasing grin. "How old did you say Miss Fairbanks is?"

Winifred pulled her reticule from her wrist and rapped him soundly on the head with it.

Chapter 3

Hannah stopped on the stone bridge to catch her breath. She had run practically all the way from St. Biddulph's, where she had spent the morning. She was expected back at Epping Hall for luncheon and there was no possible way she could make it on time. She was in the suds for sure. Her sister would be furious.

But perhaps not, she considered as she leaned against the balustrade of the bridge and rubbed at the stitch in her side. Charlotte had been *so* taken with the handsome earl that she probably had forgotten all about Hannah. Or so Hannah hoped. If not, Charlotte was sure to ring a fine peal over her head for having taken off without a word.

Hannah had left the house—or, to be perfectly honest, she had sneaked out—at an early hour without anyone taking notice. Most of the others had still been abed, though they all had retired quite early the evening before. Cousin Winifred had announced that the long, slow trip had worn them all to the bone, and so there had been only a casual cold supper laid in the dining room for those who wanted it before retiring.

But Hannah had not been exhausted. Rather, she had been itching to explore. She had bounded out of bed before sunlight and, following the spire of St. Biddulph's, had been across the river and into the village by early morning.

To her delight, St. Biddulph's was everything she had imagined and more—the most intact Saxon structure in all of Britain. She had been quite alone in her explorations until the rector had arrived and quite literally stumbled over her while she, on her hands and knees, examined the tomb effigy of a Norman knight who lay cross-legged with his feet perched on a reclining dog.

Mr. Cushing, an elderly, silver-haired, birdlike gentleman no taller than herself, had been thrilled at her interest in his church.

"It is all that remains of the eighth-century monastic settlement," he said in his curious, high-pitched voice, tinged with excitement. He was clearly pleased to have someone listen to his lecture. His parishioners probably took all this marvelous history for granted.

The rector had invited Hannah to explore at her leisure while she remained at Epping Hall, and even promised to unearth old documents regarding the church's thirteenth-century restoration for her perusal.

All things considered, it had been a perfectly lovely morning. She had been so in charity with the world that she silently thanked her sister for dragging her along to Epping Hall in the first place. Thoughts of Charlotte had reminded Hannah that she would be expected back for luncheon. A quick check of the time on the clock tower had her gathering up her notebooks, hiking up her skirts, and dashing through the church graveyard and toward the road out of the village.

"Come again! Come again!" the rector had called out in a squeaky voice while she ran. She had flung out a hand in farewell and headed toward the river.

Hannah, breathing more normally now, pushed herself away from the balustrade and continued along the bridge to the opposite side of the river. She suspected there might be time to make a thorough study of St.

Biddulph's, if she could only keep Charlotte preoccupied with the earl.

And that should pose no problem at all. The man was frightfully good-looking, and with pockets as deep as the ocean from the looks of his home. Those expressive brown eyes and gilded salons should keep Charlotte thoroughly diverted, leaving Hannah blissfully on her own.

This could turn out to be a splendid month in the country.

Gazing up to admire the bright autumn foliage, she did not see the fallen branch until she tripped on it, spilling her notebooks along the path.

"Blast!" she said, and bent down to gather up the loose papers filled with notes and drawings from St. Biddulph's.

At the sound of an approaching horse, Hannah, crouching beside a clump of gorse that had snared one of her drawings, looked over her shoulder. To her dismay, she saw a rider just clearing the bridge and heading directly for her at a fast gallop.

"Oh!" she exclaimed and stood up so that she could be seen.

"Damnation!" the rider shouted, and he pulled back on the reins so abruptly that the horse shrieked and reared wildly. "Are you all right?" he shouted in her direction.

"Yes, yes," Hannah shouted back and watched in fascinated admiration as the rider deftly and quickly attempted to bring the horse under command. They battled for a moment, but the rider controlled the reins with an expertise that showed he knew when to let the horse feel the bit. He whipped the animal around and swung it off beyond the edge of the path to calm it down. After a moment of circling and crooning to the horse, the rider dismounted and looped the reins along a tree branch.

The gentleman, for he was certainly such, removed his hat as he briskly approached her. He stopped in front of her and stared uncertainly. "Are you quite sure you are unharmed, miss?" he asked, his tone clipped and sharp, as though torn between annoyance and anxiety.

"Oh, yes," she replied and dismissed his polite concern with a wave of her hand. "But my goodness, that was excellent horsemanship, sir. How beautifully you controlled her!"

The young man gave a relieved sigh and ran a nervous hand through his sandy brown hair. "But I might have killed you," he said. "I did not see you there—"

"Oh, do not worry about that," Hannah said. "I was stupid enough to trip and drop my notebooks. I am afraid I am prone to tripping about like that. My sister tells me my mind is always in the clouds and not on my feet where it belongs." She looked down at the offending appendages that seemed to be forever causing her trouble. "Oh, and I am in the basket now, for not only am I late, but I have torn my skirt as well. Charlotte will be livid. Blast!"

She looked up to find the young gentleman staring at her with a bewildered expression. She shrugged and turned to retrieve the last of her notes from the path. "Well, I was in for it anyway, so what's a little torn muslin signify?"

The gentleman began to laugh and then bent to help her collect the papers. "I trust you will not fare too badly with your sister, miss," he said as he took the papers from her and stacked them neatly. "You may tell her that a reckless horseman knocked you to the ground through no fault of your own."

He grinned at her, and Hannah had the impression that he was some sort of rogue. She liked rogues. She envied them, actually, for they often cast propriety to the winds. Heaven only knows how often Hannah chafed under Charlotte's notions of Society's rules for young ladies. What freedom, to be a man and a rogue!

She returned the gentleman's smile with one of her own. "May I also blame you," she said, "for causing me to disappear this morning before anyone stirred and make my way to the village? And for making me late for luncheon? And for any other wrongs I may have committed so far this day?"

He laughed again. "I am at your service, miss. Blame me for anything you want. May I escort you home?"

"Oh, I am almost there," she said pointing in the general direction of the hall. "You needn't trouble yourself."

His gaze followed the direction of her own before he turned and cast her a puzzled look. "You are from Epping Hall?" At her nod, he smiled and went on. "I suppose I must expect quite a few changes since I left. It happens I am on my way to Epping as well, miss. Allow me to introduce myself. I am Major George Prescott."

"And I am Hannah Fairbanks," she said. "Prescott? You must be some relation to the earl."

"Indeed. He is my brother. I grew up at Epping."

"The earl's brother?" She looked at him more closely and called to mind the dark hair and coffee brown eyes of Lord Strickland. Beneath the sun-bleached hair and sun-darkened skin of the major were the same firm line of jaw and straight nose as his brother. And the eyes. "Ah, yes. You are very alike about the eyes," she said. "Major, eh? But where are your red coats, sir?"

He chuckled and pointed toward the horse with its heavy saddlebags. "I've sold out, you see, and come home like the prodigal son. Boney's on Elba and Nosey's troops have been disbanded. There's no more need for soldiers like me, thank the Lord. But please,

Miss Fairbanks, let me walk with you back to the hall, and you can tell me what brings you to Epping."

Hannah nodded and followed him to the horse. He took her notebooks and tucked them into a saddlebag, then untied the reins and led the mare back to the path. He asked again what brought her to Epping.

"I've come to study the architecture of St. Biddulph's," she said.

"Old St. Bidd? That musty old pile of rubble?"

"Sir!" Hannah exclaimed, outraged at such blasphemy. "It is one of, if not *the* finest example of Saxon architecture in all of Britain."

"Is it, indeed?" he said. "Who'd have thought? It always seemed a homely old lump to me, especially next to Epping."

"There is beauty in the very simplicity of Saxon and Norman structures, Major."

"I suppose," he said and gave a disinterested shrug.

Hannah could not suppress a twinge of disappointment at Major Prescott's lack of sensibility. But then, she had never really found anyone, besides Mr. Cushing, who shared her views.

"And you really came to Northamptonshire just to get a look at old St. Bidd?" he asked.

"No," she replied, "that was merely an added inducement for me to come along. You see, I've come with my sister Charlotte, Lady Abingdon, who's going to marry the earl."

Major Prescott halted abruptly and glared at her. "The devil, you say! Miles is to marry?"

"Oh, he doesn't know it yet, but my sister means to have him."

The major threw back his head and roared with laughter. "Poor Miles," he said at last. "And how long has your sister been waging this campaign?"

"We only just arrived yesterday afternoon—"

Another bark of laughter from the major.

"—but Charlotte has been planning it since Cousin Winifred suggested the idea. And now that she has seen how handsome he is . . . " Hannah clapped a hand over her mouth. "Oh, dear. I've said more than I should, haven't I? Please do not regard anything I say, Major. My tongue just gets away from me at times and—"

The major placed two gloved fingers against her lips. "Say no more, Miss Fairbanks. You need not worry that I shall repeat anything you've said." He moved his fingers, which had smelled decidedly of horse, and flashed her another roguish grin. "It will be much more entertaining to watch my unsuspecting brother succumb to Lady Abingdon's charms. She is charming, I hope? As charming as her sister?"

"Charlotte is a beauty," Hannah replied emphatically, "and a thousand times more of a real lady than I could ever hope to be."

"Do not underestimate yourself, my dear Miss Fairbanks. You have a certain charm all your own. And will no doubt blossom into as much a lady as your sister when you're older." As he smiled down at her, Hannah could have interpreted the full chronicle of his thoughts: she was just a child, grubby and uncouth, ill-mannered and unsophisticated. A child.

She had seen the same look in his brother's eyes the day before when she had alighted from the carriage and launched into that ridiculous, impulsive speech for which Charlotte had so upbraided her later. Just a child.

But Hannah was not a child. She was a woman with a woman's feelings, and it hurt her when she was dismissed as a schoolgirl. But so long as she refused to behave like a lady, to dress like a lady, she would be treated like a child. She knew it, and she didn't care. There was so much more to life than sitting quietly in a stuffy drawing room, with ankles neatly crossed and muslin crisp and uncreased. She was not interested in being a lady. She did not care what others thought of her. She did not care.

The major flicked the mare's reins and walked on. "But tell me—you did mention Cousin Winifred. Since Win is my sister, may I assume that you and I are relatives as well?"

"You may be relieved on that score, Major. You need not claim me as any sort of relation," she said in a more petulant tone than intended. It was not his fault that he had misjudged her age. She smiled up at him and modulated her tone. "It's a rather complicated sort of connection, you see. Charlotte, who is my half sister, is cousin to your sister's husband, Lord Tyndall, through her mother. I have . . . had . . . a different mother. So, though I am related to Charlotte, I am not related to Lord Tyndall. But since Charlotte has had the charge of me since my mother's death last year, Lord and Lady Tyndall very kindly asked me to come along on their visit to Epping. And because Charlotte has always referred to them as Cousin Godfrey and Cousin Winifred, I began to do the same. Rather forward of me, I suppose, but there you are."

"So Win is here, too?" the major said. "I had better brace myself for a full-scale reunion, I suppose."

"Have you been away so long, then?" Hannah asked.

"Seven years."

"Good heavens, you've not been home in all that time?"

"Afraid not," he said. "Been busy in the Peninsula."

"Were you at Toulouse?" Hannah asked with barely suppressed excitement at the possibility that the major might relate to her more details about Wellington's final battle with Napoleon's troops. This was another area about which *ladies* were supposed to be ignorant. But it had always seemed patently silly that women should not be expected to take as keen an interest in the affairs of their nation as did men. The butler at Dudley-on-the-Meese, a most obliging fellow, had always managed to smuggle the newspapers to her without Charlotte's knowing.

"Toulouse, yes. And San Sebastian and Vitoria and Ciudad Rodrigo and a dozen other such minor skirmishes as I recall."

"My goodness," Hannah said as she closely surveyed the man at her side and wondered how any man could have survived so much battle and still maintain a sense of humor. Soldiers were a strange and wonderful breed apart. She had known an officer in Dudley who'd lost an arm at Salamanca and had sported his empty sleeve with pride. "And yet you seem to have survived intact," she said. "You appear to have all your parts."

The major laughed. "It appears so." His voice sobered as he added, "I have been lucky. Extremely lucky. Others . . . others were not so fortunate."

"Are you just now returned from Toulouse?" Hannah asked.

"I came back in June with old Nosey," he replied. "Been celebrating the peace in London ever since."

"You've been in England all these months and have not come home to see your family?"

He shrugged, gave her a sheepish smile, and turned onto the gravel path leading to Epping's stables. "I saw Miles in London in June. But I was not ready to come home just yet."

Hannah studied him and decided he did not look the sort to play the hero. He did not even wear his uniform. There must be some other reason that kept him away from Epping. "Well, I am sure it is none of my business," she said, "but I suspect the earl and Lady Tyndall will be very pleased to see you home at last.

And I am also sure that Charlotte will make a big fuss over you, especially if you put on your red coats."

"Shall I make a grand entrance, then," he said, "and divert attention from your tardy return?"

"Oh, splendid!" Hannah said as he led the horse into the stable. "I knew you were a right one. Even if you don't know beans about architecture."

Miles sat in his study and surveyed the account books before him. At the sound of a knock on the door, he replied, "Come," without looking away from the rows of figures.

"Hello, Miles."

Miles's head jerked up at the sound of the familiar voice. His younger brother stood just inside the doorway, grinning sheepishly. "Good God, George. Is it really you?"

"The prodigal returns," George said, and flopped down into a comfortable leather chair opposite the desk.

Miles stood and walked around his desk to clap his brother fondly on the shoulder. "I wondered when you would get around to coming home," he said, and then leaned against the desk and crossed his arms over his chest. "When we met in London, I wasn't sure if you'd ever get up the nerve."

"The nerve?" George looked as if he were ready to leap out of his chair.

Miles held up a conciliatory hand. "Steady on, old boy. No offense meant. But I know, at least I think I know, how difficult it will be for you to face her again."

George settled back into the chair and gave a mirthless snort of laughter. "Difficult," he muttered. "Yes, well, I have faced worse situations in the last seven years."

"And even this one could be worse, you know,"

Miles said. "She could be married with a brood of noisy children."

"Oh, no. That would not be worse, brother. That would be easy. At least I would know where I stand and could get on with things. But the way it is . . . Why the devil has she not married, Miles? She is five-and-twenty, for God's sake. She should be married. Has she had offers?"

"Joseph has never mentioned any," Miles replied. "But then I do not believe Rachel has given encouragement to any particular gentleman. I suspect she has waited for you, George."

"No. No, she would not. We parted bitterly. She was not willing to forgive me. She would not have waited."

"Well, whether or not she has been waiting for your return, the fact is she is unmarried. Firmly on the shelf, Winifred would say. What do you intend to do?"

"I don't know. I don't know how I feel about her anymore. Seven years is a long time. I've seen and done things I could never have imagined. I am not the same arrogant young pup I was then. Rachel and I will have nothing in common anymore. I will stay for only a short visit and then be on my way. It is time I tended to the estate father left me. It has been too long neglected."

"Well, your arrival could not have been better timed," Miles said. "Winifred and Godfrey are here. They will be very pleased to see you. And they have brought along two of Godfrey's cousins."

"Yes, I know," George said. Miles gave his brother a quizzical look. "I met the most enchanting young girl on the road from the village," George explained. "Hannah Fairbanks."

"Ah. So that's where she disappeared to this morning."

"She is quite an engaging child, Miles. A breath of fresh air, in fact. Oh, to be so young again!"

"Winifred will be quick to inform you that she is not the child she seems. She is almost twenty, apparently."

"You're joking?"

"Not a bit. And there's the older sister as well. A widow."

"Ah yes. Lady Abingdon." George cast his brother a wicked grin. "Miss Fairbanks mentioned her."

"Hmph." Miles was not at all comfortable with the look in George's eyes. "Be on your guard, my boy," he said, "or Winifred will get her matchmaking claws into you before you know what's hit you. She does not know about what happened between you and Rachel. And you're the perfect age for Miss Fairbanks."

"Good God."

"And I should further warn you that Joseph is staying at Epping as well."

"Joseph?"

"Yes. I invited him to even out the numbers when I heard that Winifred was bringing along two ladies. Had I known you were coming there would have been no need. You would be the natural escort for the engaging Miss Fairbanks," Miles added with a grin.

The brothers chatted for another half hour about the estate, about family, about all that had happened during George's absence. The new arrival was shown to his room by a beaming Mrs. Harvey. After a change of clothes, he joined the rest of the party in the drawing room where tea was being served.

Winifred threw her arms around her brother and cried into his neckcloth. Godfrey pumped his hand enthusiastically and clapped him on the back at every opportunity, saying, "Good to see you. Good to see you." Joseph Wetherby was equally effusive in his welcome, though he did cast a wary glance or two in Miles's direction.

After being introduced to Lady Abingdon, George joined his brother on one of the red velvet settees.

"What a fortunate fellow you are, Miles," he said in an undertone when all the others appeared to be deeply involved in a conversation on the upcoming hunting season. "Lady Abingdon is indeed a beauty. To have such a woman thrown in your path, Miles, will make you the envy of every warm-blooded male in the county. Her sister told me as much. By the way, where is Miss Fairbanks?"

"I haven't the faintest idea," Miles replied. "I've not seen her all day."

"Lady Abingdon is not the most dutiful of chaperones, then, is she?"

"I believe she finds Miss Fairbanks a trial," Miles said, "or at least that is what Winifred has said. Despairs of successfully launching the girl into Society."

"—and it is all your fault, George, for showing up unannounced."

Both brothers looked up at the sound of their sister's voice.

"What is my fault?" George asked.

"That our numbers are now uneven again. You know how I abhor uneven numbers. We must add another female to our little gathering. But who, on such short notice?" After the briefest of pauses and before anyone else had a chance to offer a suggestion, Winifred clapped her hands together eagerly. "But of course," she said with enthusiasm. "Rachel Wetherby. I am sure she can have no other plans. Joseph, do dash on home and bring her along, will you?"

Miles felt George stiffen next to him and intercepted an awkward glance from Joseph.

"I . . . I am not sure my sister is free," Joseph said. "She may have—"

"Of course she is free," Winifred said. "Spinsters are always free."

"But Winifred," Miles said, "perhaps she may not—"

"She must get used to being asked to make up numbers," Winifred said. "That is the unfortunate lot of spinsters, and Rachel has chosen that role for herself. I am sure she might have married many times over these last several years if she had wanted. But she did not. And so now she must make herself available to others. Please go and get her at once, Joseph."

George rose from the settee and brushed away a piece of nonexistent lint from the sleeve of his jacket. "That won't be necessary, Win," he said. "I do not plan to stay. Do not add to your number on my account."

"Not stay? Not stay?" Winifred's voice had risen to a high-pitched squeal. "Well, of course you mean to stay. You have not been to Epping in seven years, George. I will not have you running off so soon. You will stay the month while we are here."

"I am sorry, Win, but I—"

"Don't be absurd, George," Winifred said. "You must stay. Miles, tell him he must stay."

Miles rose and turned to face his brother. "Winifred is right, George. It is too long since we have seen you. I will try to convince him to stay, Winifred. Perhaps when he meets his nieces for the first time, they will charm him into staying. Come, George. It is time you met my daughters."

George gave him a grateful look as Miles led him out of the drawing room. "Good God, I had forgotten what an unstoppable force Win can be," George whispered.

Miles chuckled. "Wellington could have used her, I am sure."

"Indeed," George replied, "the frogs would have run screaming. But how can I remain here, Miles, if Rachel is invited to stay? I don't know if I can—"

"You must face her eventually, George. Best to get it over with. Besides, if things between you go well, then you will have the pleasure of each other's company every day, under the same roof."

"And if they do not go well?"

"My lord?" The soft voice caused the brothers to stop and turn around. Lady Abingdon approached them from the corridor outside the drawing room, the fine green muslin of her skirts swishing about her in a graceful flutter as she walked toward them. "If you do not mind," she said, "I, too, would be pleased to meet your daughters, Lord Strickland. I do so love children."

For some reason, the love of children was one of the last virtues Miles would have assigned to Lady Abingdon. But that was not fair. Winifred had told him she had no children of her own. Perhaps she was genuinely interested. In any case, she would have to meet the girls sooner or later—especially if he was to begin a serious courtship. And if she continued to speak to him in that intriguingly seductive whisper, he would be ready and eager to begin that courtship at any moment.

Somehow, as he looked at her, he suspected that was precisely what she intended.

"Of course, Lady Abingdon," he said. "I would be pleased to introduce you to my daughters. How kind of you to ask."

George stepped aside to allow the lady to pass and gave his brother a wink that said he, too, knew what she was up to.

Miles led them upstairs to the nursery. "Though the girls have heard all about their uncle," he said for the benefit of Lady Abingdon, "they have never before met him. They are convinced you are quite the hero, George. You ought to have worn your red coats."

"You are the second person today to tell me so. But truly, I am just as anxious to meet my nieces," George said. "Your letters were full of them. Do you recall the picture you sent that Amy drew for me when she was—what?—three? It always made me smile and remember what I was fighting for. I kept it with me at all times. I still have it, in fact."

Miles came to an abrupt stop in the corridor leading to the nursery. The other two were forced to come to a halt to avoid a collision. Miles looked at his brother in surprise, never thinking him the sentimental sort. "You still have it?" he asked.

"Right here." George reached into one of his waist-coat pockets and drew out a folded piece of parchment. "A bit the worse for wear," he continued as he unfolded the frayed sheet carefully, "but relatively intact."

He held out a faded and cracked painted picture of a large-headed figure with a round red body and black stick legs and arms. The letters A M Y were awkwardly scrawled across the bottom.

"Good heavens, I remember this," Miles said as a flurry of memories raced through his head. Tiny, blond-haired Amy, the very picture of her mother, making the serious effort to paint a picture of her unknown uncle, the soldier. Amelia, weak and frail in her sickbed, hugging Amy and promising to have it sent to Uncle George in Spain. Amy watching carefully while Miles addressed the letter.

Was it only two years ago?

"Do you suppose Amy will remember painting it?" George asked.

"I am certain she will," Miles replied. "But you must show it to her and see for yourself."

The three of them walked to the nursery door and halted at the sound of shouts and shrieks of laughter. "Ah," Miles said, "the twins always have that effect on my otherwise delightfully well-behaved daughters." He smiled at Lady Abingdon. "I hope you will take this first impression with a grain of salt, my lady. Those two young hellions can wreak total havoc in slightly less than two minutes."

"As I am well aware, Lord Strickland," she replied with a mocking smile. "You must recall that I spent several days on the road with them."

"Yes, of course," he said. "Then you will forgive the unnaturally high spirits of my two little ones."

"Winifred's boys?" George asked. "Hellions, you say? Good Lord, they were not even yet walking when I left."

"You have missed a great deal, old chap," Miles said, and flashed his brother a wicked grin. "Let us ensure that you begin making up for lost time . . . right now." He opened the door to the nursery.

And stood rooted to the spot at the sight before him.

All four children were climbing a mock mountain made of . . . Miss Fairbanks.

The girl was sprawled on the floor on hands and knees with her bottom thrust high in the air and a great deal of shapely leg exposed. Tiny Caro, his youngest daughter, not quite three, climbed to the top of the peak formed by Miss Fairbanks and slid down the girl's back with squeals of delight.

The now familiar sound of Lady Abingdon's outraged gasp was followed by a crack of laughter from George.

Shouts from the children alerted Miss Fairbanks to the presence of visitors. Her face, pressed to the floor, turned to catch the eye of her sister.

"Hannah!" Lady Abingdon exclaimed in as loud a voice as Miles had ever heard her use. "What are you doing? How can you be so childish and unladylike in the company of our host? Get off the floor this instant."

George continued to snicker, and Miles himself was hard pressed to keep a smile off his face. He wanted to turn to Lady Abingdon and tell her to ease up on the girl, that she was merely entertaining the children. But her anger was almost palpable, and Miles decided this was not a battle he cared to enter. This was between the two sisters.

But the children, including his own little girls, were clearly having a wonderful time, and for that he was grateful. He did not care how unconventional Miss Fairbanks was in her manners, or how she disported herself in the nursery. At the moment, he was utterly charmed by the whole rowdy group of them, and found himself considering the very uncharacteristic notion of joining them on the floor.

Reaching up to finger the pristine linen at his throat, he regained control of himself, and the notion was squelched.

Miss Fairbanks rolled up and sat back on her knees. Her stocking-clad toes peeked out from behind. Unruly brown curls spilled down her back in charming, lopsided disarray as most of her hairpins had become dislodged.

"Hello, Charlotte, my lord, Major Prescott." She appeared not the least embarrassed, not in any way cowed by her sister's anger. She sat back and pulled her feet forward, then twisted about until she was sitting cross-legged. And Miles was astonished to see his eldest daughter—quiet, petulant, solitary Amy—scamper onto Miss Fairbanks's lap as if it were the most natural thing in the world. The young woman hugged Amy close to her and smiled up at Miles.

"What wonderful daughters you have, my lord. We have been having a splendid time, haven't we, Amy?"

Amy nodded her head energetically and began to giggle. This sad little girl, who had never quite understood why her mother had been taken away, actually giggled.

And Miles's heart melted at the sight.

Chapter 4

Men were stupid creatures, Hannah decided as she watched the earl and Mr. Wetherby chatting with Charlotte on the other side of the drawing room as they waited for dinner to be announced. How easily they fell victim to her sister's manufactured charm. They appeared completely captivated. Charlotte had their undivided attention as she spoke to them in her whispery for-gentlemen-only voice.

Only a complete dolt would fail to understand what she was doing.

If those two men had an ounce of sense between them they would have said, "I beg your pardon, Lady Abingdon, I am afraid I didn't catch that. Would you mind speaking up a bit?" But, no. They did not. Men never did. They did precisely what Charlotte hoped they would do. They leaned in closer, giving her their full attention so as not to miss a single whispered word. Close enough to appreciate the special jasmine fragrance she wore. Close enough to touch. The poor fools had to concentrate so hard in order to hear what she said that everyone and everything else was forgotten. They were hers.

"Just look at them" she muttered.

"Look at whom?"

Hannah turned to find Major Prescott at her side. Good heavens, had she really spoken her thoughts aloud? Again? Would she never learn to curb her tongue?

"Do you mean Miles and Wetherby?" the major continued. "All right, then. I'm looking. Just what is it, exactly, that I am supposed to observe? How they cannot tear their eyes from your charming sister, perhaps?"

Hannah gave an unladylike snort.

"Come now, Miss Fairbanks. Surely you are not jealous of your own sister?"

"What foolishness," she said.

"Indeed. You have no cause to be jealous, my dear." He reached out and gently tucked a stray curl of hair behind her ear. Blast those wretched hair pins. Why would they never stay in place? "You have considerable charms of your own," the major said, "as any gentleman here will tell you. Granted, yours are not so . . . so practiced as those of Lady Abingdon. But there is often more appeal in artless innocence."

"Artless? Ha! Only this afternoon you thought me an uncouth schoolgirl. Oh, do not deny it," she said as he began to protest. "You know it is true. But it doesn't signify. Everyone who meets me mistakes me for a child." She looked down and absently shuffled one foot back and forth. She noted that somehow she had already managed to scuff the toe of one of her new striped slippers. "It is my own fault," she muttered in an undertone.

"Whatever impression I may have given this afternoon," the major said, "I assure you, my dear Miss Fairbanks, that I find you a lovely and charming young lady. Especially," he said and briefly ran his fingertips along the sleeve of her gown, "in that particular shade of blue. Or aquamarine, or whatever you ladies call it. It accentuates your beautiful blue eyes."

The idiot, Hannah thought, and took the major by the elbow and led him slightly away from the others gathered in the drawing room. It was such an enormous room that there was no problem establishing a bit of distance in order to have a private conversation. She glanced briefly in the direction of Cousin Winifred, who was chatting with Miss Wetherby, the most recent arrival and the sister of the jovial Mr. Wetherby. Unlike her gregarious brother, Rachel Wetherby seemed quiet, rather prim, and terribly uncomfortable. She darted a glance toward the major, then caught Hannah's eye and turned away.

"This will not do, Major Prescott," Hannah said. "It won't work."

"I beg your pardon? What won't work?"

"Flirting with me. It will never make her jealous."

The major stiffened.

"For one thing," Hannah continued, "it's too obvious. Especially when your glance strays in Miss Wetherby's direction every time you are supposedly flirting with me. And for another thing, I'm not the sort men flirt with, so that dog won't hunt. Besides, why choose me to make someone jealous when you could easily have my sister hanging all over you? But you've likely been told not to interfere with your brother's plans in that quarter. I suppose I am the only other female available to you." She sighed and shook her head. "Well, it won't work, Major. You will never make her jealous with me."

His dark eyes glared at her with an intensity that must have sent his troops scrambling to do his bidding. "I have no idea what you are talking about, Miss Fairbanks."

"Oh, bosh. Do you think me a complete flat?" She had lowered her voice to a conspiratorial whisper. "It's as plain as the nose on your face that you're out to make Miss Wetherby jealous," Hannah said. "I cannot imagine why—she looks for all the world like a governess. I suppose she is rather pretty, though, isn't she, in a quiet sort of way. If only she would smile more often."

"Miss Fairbanks—"

"Why on earth would you want to make such a woman jealous? I would wager you haven't laid eyes on her in seven years. Oh! Oh, but that's it, isn't it?" Hannah gave a triumphant smile when the major furrowed his brow. "I thought there must have been something other than London parties keeping you away from home when you'd finally returned to England after so many years. She's the reason you have stayed away so long, isn't she? And why you felt so reluctant to come home. You've some sort of history together, have you not?"

"Miss Fairbanks—"

"Oh, do not worry, Major." She lowered her voice again and turned away from the others gathered in the drawing room. "Your secret is safe with me," she continued, and made a show of admiring the huge family portrait that dominated one end of the room. Her supposed interest would perhaps offer an explanation for her dragging the major away from the others. And it was not a completely spurious maneuver. The painting was likely a Van Dyck and, though not to her taste, certainly impressive. "But it won't be a secret much longer," she went on, "if the two of you continue to make such prodigious efforts to avoid one another."

The major chuckled. "You did warn me, Miss Fairbanks," he said, "that your tongue gets away from you at times."

"Oh, dear. I've done it again, haven't I?"

The major grinned.

"Well, you see what a hopeless case I am? Not exactly worthy of a flirtation, am I?" Hannah laughed aloud at the very idea. "Setting up as your flirt an *artless* girl who never seems to know when to keep her tongue between her teeth? You do not imagine that anyone would believe it for a moment, do you? And Miss Wetherby is no green girl to fall for such nonsense. Give it up, Major. It won't fadge."

Major Prescott gave such a bark of laughter that heads turned in their direction. Hannah peeked over her shoulder and intercepted a glowering look from Charlotte.

"My dear Miss Fairbanks, you are quite remarkable. I do not recall ever before having a woman sincerely object to a bit of flirtation."

"Oh, I do not object to it on principle, you understand," Hannah said. "In other circumstances it would be quite flattering, I assure you. But at the moment it just seems silly when the true object of your interest is someone else. Why not flirt with her?"

"Oh, I don't think so."

"Why ever not?"

"It's a long story, Miss Fairbanks."

"Oh, do call me Hannah. And you needn't tell me your long story. I can make up one of my own that is likely close enough to the truth. But in my opinion, which I am sure is not worth a ha'penny token, you would do better to speak with her rather than trying to make her jealous."

"Do you really think so?" The major's tone had become remarkably diffident, and he stole yet another glance in the direction of Miss Wetherby.

Hannah smiled at the gaping crack in this soldier's armor. "I may be far off the mark," she said, "since I really have no experience in these matters. But if it were me you had an awkward history with, I am sure I would rather have you face me straight on than play silly games to make me jealous. Besides, you will have to speak with her eventually. Even if it's likely to be uncomfortable, it's probably best to get it out of the way, don't you think?"

The major smiled and reached out to straighten yet

another of Hannah's wayward curls. "You are wise for one so young, Miss Fairbanks."

"It's Hannah. And I may be sending you into an ambush, so don't think me so clever just yet."

Miles did not know what to think of Lady Abingdon. She was very beautiful and surrounded by some sort of exotic fragrance that was almost intoxicating. In the years before his marriage, before he had met Amelia, he would not have thought twice about taking such a woman to his bed.

But she was not here as a potential mistress, and they both knew it. And as a potential wife, he would not treat her with such disrespect, as much as she seemed to invite it. And that was the problem. She was the most seductive creature he'd ever met. He did not know whether it was natural or practiced, inadvertent or deliberate, but it was certainly disconcerting, and had more than once threatened to crack his well-honed lord-of-the-manor demeanor. When he had considered the benefits of taking an older, experienced woman, a widow, as his second wife, he had not counted on this particular benefit. He should be thrilled. But somehow the whole idea set his teeth on edge.

He was out of practice. That was the problem. He had married young and kept himself here in the country most of the year, with his sheep and his tenant farms and his family. He had made only one foray into Society since Amelia's death and had made a perfect fool of himself.

At the Chissingworth house party, he had concentrated on courting a young girl no older than Miss Fairbanks. He now wished he had not ignored all the silent, and some not so silent, invitations from various older women during the party. Had he allowed himself a bit of dalliance at Chissingworth, he might have

been better prepared for Lady Abingdon's open flirtation.

But perhaps not. After all, she was not here for a bit
of dalliance, but potentially for something much more
serious. What did it really matter if she used a bit of seduction to reach her goal, which was, in the end, the
same as his own? It wasn't what he was used to. It certainly wasn't what he had planned. But what did it
matter? Perhaps he was simply too punctilious for his
own good. He wondered when he had become such a
straitlaced old prig.

He watched the lovely widow as she replied to
some remark of Joseph's. George was right. Miles
should consider himself a fortunate fellow. She was
beautiful. She was seductive.

And he was out of practice.

"I say, Miles?"

He wrenched his gaze from the beautiful widow to
find George standing before him with Miss Fairbanks
at his side. He had noted earlier that the girl had made
an attempt to look more grown-up this evening. Or
perhaps it was not exactly a conscious attempt. Perhaps it was just that she wore a very pretty dress and
had arranged her hair in a mass of curls atop her head
that made her look more her true age. But even as he
watched, one of those curls threatened to tumble
down her neck, and he could not help but recall how
she had looked in the nursery earlier that afternoon.
He suppressed a grin at the memory.

"Miss Fairbanks has expressed an interest in the Van
Dycks," George said. Miss Fairbanks shot a startled
look at George, but masked it with a wan smile when
she realized Miles had seen it. "You know I could
never keep them all straight, " George continued, "so I
thought perhaps you might point out for her all the
important ones, and explain who's who and all that."

Miles rose and deftly adjusted the tails of his jacket.

He offered a smile to Miss Fairbanks, who, he suspected, had little interest in the famous paintings. "It would be my pleasure," he said. He excused himself to Lady Abingdon, who looked none too pleased, and Joseph, who looked delighted. Miles offered his arm to Miss Fairbanks. She grinned, revealing her dimples, raised her brows in a smug look-at-me expression aimed at her sister, and took his arm. He guided her back toward the large family portrait.

"This is the fourth Earl of Strickland with his wife, children, and grandchildren" Miles said. "It was painted by Van Dyck in the 1630s, as were all the other portraits in the room."

"They are all quite splendid," Miss Fairbanks said. "And this part of the house was designed about that time as well?"

"Ah. I had forgotten you are a student of architecture. I suspect the dimensions of the room hold more interest for you than do the paintings."

Miss Fairbanks smiled and hunched a shoulder. "Yes, but the paintings are so much a part of the room, aren't they? It is almost as if—"

"The room was designed especially to display them?"

"Yes. Was it, then? By Inigo Jones?"

"Indeed. Have you studied the work of Jones?" Miles asked.

"Only a bit," she replied. "In books. I've never actually seen anything designed by him until now. I haven't ventured much out of Shropshire, you see."

"And what do you think of your first Jones building?"

Her brow furrowed, and she chewed on her lower lip. She clearly wrestled for an appropriate answer, and the struggle played itself out across her face like a battle. After her embarrassingly plain speaking the day before, he would not have expected her to so carefully consider her response.

"The classic proportions of the room are quite noble," she said at last. "But, to be perfectly honest with you, my lord, all that gilt and carved decoration is a bit overpowering. If you don't mind my saying so, I really cannot imagine how you manage to live amongst all this . . . this baroque splendor."

Miles smiled. She had managed to be quite blunt after all. "I can see how you might feel that way, Miss Fairbanks. But I assure you, it is only the public rooms and the state bedrooms that are maintained in this style. I think you will find the private quarters much more subdued."

"Oh, yes. My own bedchamber is quite charming, I thank you. And on my way out this morning—for a walk—I poked my head into a library or study on the ground floor. Believe me, if I had not been in such a hurry I could have curled up like a cat in that room. It looked terribly comfortable and warm and inviting."

"Ah. My study."

"Oh! I did not mean to intrude into a private room. I am so sorry. I promise you I will not—"

"You may use the study any time you wish, Miss Fairbanks. There is a rather large collection of books you might enjoy, many on architecture. I even have some of Inigo Jones's original drawings for Epping. You are welcome to look at them at any time."

"Oh, I should love that! Thank you ever so much. Do you by chance have anything on the local Norman and Saxon architecture?"

"I'm not sure. Perhaps. I shall have a look around and see what I can find. But if there aren't any books, you can make do with the real thing. St. Biddulph's, just across the river, is—"

"Oh, I know!" Her face positively lit up with excitement. "Is it not marvelous? I declare, it is the most beautiful thing I have ever seen!"

Miles glanced about at the room described by guide books as one of the most beautiful rooms in all of England, then mentally compared it to the plain, dumpy little Saxon church in the village. To each her own, he supposed. "You've been to St. Bidd's already?" he asked.

She grinned sheepishly. "That's where I went this morning, you see. I could hardly wait and so dashed out before anyone was the wiser. I spent the whole morning there." She leaned in closer and lowered her voice. "But please don't tell Lottie."

"Lottie?"

"My sister. Charlotte. Oh, and don't tell her I called her Lottie either. She hates that."

"All right," he said with a sober nod of the head, keeping his amusement in check. "I won't tell. But why should she care that you've been to see the church?"

"Oh, she wants me to stay indoors and engage in demure conversation and practice acting like a lady."

"Practice?"

"For the next Season. She means to fire me off, you see." She gave a little snort. "Absurd."

"Why absurd?" he asked, wondering how it was he had allowed the conversation to branch off into such inappropriate territory. "Are you not interested in having a Season, and perhaps—"

"Landing a husband? No, my lord, I am *not* interested. In fact, I am hoping some other relative will conveniently pop off in the next few months so I can go back into mourning and avoid the whole thing. And perhaps a whole string of obliging relations will contrive to keep me in black gloves until I am old enough to be left quietly on the shelf."

Miles wanted to laugh aloud at this brash pronouncement. It was difficult to maintain his usual restraint in the company of this unconventional girl and her unabashed manner. He quickly brought himself under control, but allowed himself a smile. "What a gruesome young woman you are, to be sure, Miss Fairbanks. Thank heavens I am not one of your relations. I should be afraid for my life."

She grinned up at him, dimples winking. "I am only joking, my lord, as I am sure you must know. But if you *do* happen to establish a connection between us"—she arched a brow and darted a glance in the direction of her sister—"you may rest assured that your life will not be threatened. I promise to keep my distance."

Though her tone was still teasing, some other emotion flickered across her eyes during that last statement. He wondered what it was, but was more distracted by the realization that everyone expected him to marry Lady Abingdon. It was apparently considered to be a fait accompli. And though it felt akin to being swept up in a tide, he did not feel the urge to fight it. He knew it was entirely likely he would marry the beautiful widow. But if he did, he hoped that Miss Fairbanks would not keep her distance. She was much too delightful.

"You set my mind at ease, Miss Fairbanks. But tell me about your visit to old St. Bidd's. Did you happen to meet Mr. Cushing?"

"Indeed. And he was very kind and showed me all about."

"He's been rector there since I was a boy. He's quite a scholar, you know." She met his gaze squarely, with curiosity and no hint of guile, encouraging him to tell her more. "When we were children," he continued, "Mr. Cushing used to give us all lectures on the history of the place. But Winifred and George and our other brother, Nigel, used to sneak away. They all seemed to accept our father's view of history, which was that it began when Henry the Eighth granted the land and earldom to one of our Prescott ancestors. Nothing before that time was of any importance."

Miss Fairbanks tilted her head and stared up at him with candid blue eyes. Whether she wanted it or not, he suspected those eyes, with their long dark lashes and clear blue depths, would land her a husband eventually, Season or no Season. "But you did not agree, did you?" she said. "You were interested in what Mr. Cushing had to say."

"Yes, I'm afraid I was always the dullest of my father's children," Miles said. "As a boy, I loved exploring the old church while my siblings preferred riding and hunting. We were all blooded early, but I got a bigger thrill rushing to tell Mr. Cushing when I thought I'd discovered a Roman carving built into one of the doorjambs."

"Yes, there are many ancient fragments used in the original Saxon walls. Mr. Cushing showed me the slim Roman bricks in the nave arches, though of course I'd read about them and would have recognized them anyway. They stand out so clearly against the other masonry."

She chattered on enthusiastically about the various architectural characteristics of the old church. It was easy enough to get caught up in her excitement. He had always loved St. Bidd's, more from a sense of personal attachment than from any sort of academic appreciation. Though it had been a place of discovery when he was a child, as an adult he was connected to it on a more emotional level. He had been married there. His children had been christened there. His wife was buried there. As were his parents, grandparents, and countless other Prescotts.

He had never really thought about the church in terms of any sort of architectural importance. Living in the Palladian masterpiece that was Epping Hall, one tended to forget other sites of historical importance.

He was frankly fascinated as Miss Fairbanks extolled the significance of the surviving Saxon features of St. Biddulph's. She evidently knew what she was talking about. Clearly, she was a scholar. Her blue eyes flashed with a fervent passion for her subject, and he found himself wondering how he had ever believed her to be a child.

That thought reminded him that he had wanted to say something to her about his own children. To thank her for spending time with them, for playing with them, for making them laugh.

But before he could interrupt her to do so, dinner was announced. Since it was a small, informal family gathering, they did not stand on ceremony in terms of who escorted whom into the dining room. The proper order of precedence was disregarded on such occasions, and Miles decided, uncharacteristically, to keep Miss Fairbanks on his arm.

She continued to chatter on about plans to explore the sunken ambulatory at St. Biddulph's as he steered her toward the dining room. Godfrey had offered his arm to Lady Abingdon. Miles caught her eye and smiled. He then noticed that Rachel Wetherby had taken George's arm. She did not smile. Miles tried to catch his brother's eye, but George had eyes only for Rachel. Perhaps things would work out for them this time. He hoped so. He knew, though she would never admit it, that Rachel had indeed waited all these years for George to return. He hoped his brother would not disappoint her again.

Chapter 5

Hannah wished they would all go away. A thousand questions danced on the tip of her tongue, but she was trying her best to keep quiet. She knew that only Lord Strickland would be able to provide answers, and Charlotte had him firmly attached to her side at the moment. Her sister would be seriously displeased if Hannah distracted the earl by peppering him with questions. She had scolded Hannah soundly the night before for supposedly monopolizing him.

Hannah had done no such thing. She was not the one who had flirted outrageously with the earl throughout the evening. She was not the one who had encouraged him to stroll with her on the terrace while the rest of them played cards. She was not the one who had disappeared with the man for half an hour.

All Hannah had done was talk with him. She liked him. She had expected him to be stuffy, despite being younger and better-looking that she had expected. He was an earl, after all. He should be stuffy.

But he was not. True, he had a slightly formal manner when he was in a group, and seemed always to be conscious of his position as host. But when she had spoken to him alone he had seemed perfectly ordinary. Well, not ordinary, perhaps. But he was friendly and interesting, and he had listened to her. Really listened. One could tell because there was such an intensity about his dark eyes. He listened with his eyes, silently encouraging her to rattle on about St. Biddulph's. But he loved the old church, too, she could tell. And so she knew he was not merely being polite.

At least she hoped he was not. His impeccable manners had no doubt been bred in him from the cradle, along with rank, duty, honor, and all the other noble qualities that oozed from every pore. But she was sure his interest had been genuine.

Or perhaps he simply appreciated a few moments of intelligent conversation.

She would wager her new striped slippers that Charlotte had not engaged him in any sort of serious conversation. She did not like to think what her sister *had* engaged him in during that half hour.

But that was no concern of Hannah's. Charlotte was going to marry the man, after all.

Which meant that Charlotte would have him all to herself for years to come. Which meant that she should not begrudge Hannah a few moments of conversation with him. And she had so many questions!

Lord Strickland had invited Charlotte and Hannah on a tour of the exterior of Epping Hall and its grounds. The rest of the party, all of whom knew Epping well and needed no tour, were nevertheless invited along for the exercise. The day was autumn crisp and clear; the elm and ash trees in all their reds and golds dotted the sweeping green lawns surrounding the house. Everyone was eager to join in, except for Cousin Godfrey, who opted to stay indoors. Hannah suspected his plans included stretching out on one of the sofas for a long nap.

Hannah's interest in the house surprised her. But she had studied the work of Andrea Palladio and could not fail to appreciate his influence on seventeenth-century British architecture. But it was not only the Palladian designs of Inigo Jones that intrigued her. There were hints of an older structure as well that piqued Hannah's interest. And she had never before been to such a large and imposing estate. It was all quite new to her, and there was so much she wanted to know.

But she could not hear all of the earl's commentary because Charlotte had led him apart while the others lagged behind. Neither the major nor Winifred could provide her with the sort of information she sought. Each time she asked a question, she received the same sort of answer.

"I suppose," Winifred said when asked about one of the corner towers, "that it might have been part of Jones's construction in the seventeenth century, as you suggest. Or perhaps it was part of the eighth Earl's additions in the mid-eighteenth century. To tell you the truth, I haven't the slightest idea. George, do you recall?"

The major neither recalled nor cared. He was completely absorbed in quiet conversation with Miss Wetherby. Hannah was pleased to see he had taken her advice. Miss Wetherby remained reserved and somewhat aloof, but at least they were talking.

And then Hannah caught Miss Wetherby scowling in her direction. A wink from the major was all she needed to realize that, although he was no longer avoiding Miss Wetherby, he had not completely given up the notion of using Hannah to make her jealous. Hannah wondered, somewhat uncomfortably, what sort of foolish things he might be saying about her.

But that was not important at the moment. The really burning question, the thing that mattered most, was the origin of the corner tower.

"You must ask Miles," Winifred said for perhaps the third time. "He knows all about such things." But it was clear she meant that Hannah should ask him later. With little more than a slight twist of her body, she indicated that the earl and Charlotte should be left alone.

It was Winifred, after all, who had encouraged their courtship in the first place. Like Charlotte, she wanted no interference.

And so the questions continued to pile up in her brain like firewood until Hannah was positively itching to speak to Lord Strickland.

An opportunity presented itself in the most natural manner before she could contrive of one herself. Mr. Wetherby and Winifred were chuckling over some town gossip.

"I heard," Mr. Wetherby said, "that it happened at Lady Endicott's rout, but I cannot recall if it was Lord Wortham or Lord Teesdale."

Hannah, who had not been paying attention and really had no idea what they were talking about, was nevertheless unwilling to miss this opening.

"I believe Charlotte is a friend of Lady Endicott's," she said with perfect truthfulness. "Perhaps you should ask her."

And he did. Mr. Wetherby called out to Charlotte before Winifred could stop him. Charlotte turned away from Lord Strickland with obvious reluctance and joined the others. But she was a social creature at heart. She loved London and the Season and Society, and was easily drawn into the sort of conversation that was second nature to her. In no time at all she was laughing with the others over whatever bit of scandal-broth they had stirred up.

Then it was the most natural thing in the world for Hannah to approach Lord Strickland. He stood alone, some distance apart from the others, near one of the ancient larch trees that flanked the house. Tall and impeccably dressed, almost imposing in his dignity, Hannah ought to have checked herself but did not.

"I am curious, my lord," she said without preamble, "to know whether or not the central section of this wing is actually Tudor?"

"I might have known your educated eye would recognize it," the earl said. "You are quite correct, Miss Fairbanks." He smiled with obvious pleasure at her show of interest.

Charlotte had no doubt feigned interest badly. Or perhaps she did not even try, and spoke of more frivolous things instead, as she was given to do in the presence of gentlemen. "Put your books away, my girl," she had said to Hannah on more than one occasion. "Never let a gentleman believe you to have a brain. They are insecure creatures at best and are threatened by the very idea of an intelligent woman."

What rot.

"That portion," the earl continued, "along with the porch in the inner courtyard, are all that is left of the original Tudor manor house. Jones had intended to leave it intact and flank it with wings matching his new southern front. But that never happened, and the existing wings were constructed some decades later by another architect."

"I am glad it was left intact," Hannah said. "It is tall and proud—an impressive entrance. I especially like the oriel window."

"Do you?" Hannah looked up to find Lord Strickland smiling at her, and a distinct twinkle in those brown eyes. She had got an impression the night before of the sense of humor lurking beneath that rigid lord-of-the-manor bearing. She was pleased to discover she had not been wrong. "I did not believe you admired anything quite so modern," he said.

She laughed. "I do on occasion admire something outside of the medieval. Not often, mind you. But I do admire Epping Hall. It is quite beautiful."

"And I thought you thoroughly put off by the extravagant interiors." His brows beetled into a disapproving scowl, but the eyes retained their twinkle.

"Well," Hannah said, "if you must know, I do admire the exterior more. It is serene and noble. The lines are clean. Very little ornamentation. All in all, it is very pleasing on the eye, my lord."

"So I have always thought," he said softly. His gaze swept slowly along the length of the wing before them, then returned to her. "But I suppose I should not be surprised that it appeals to you, Miss Fairbanks. Its plan is as simple as any medieval keep. Four-square, compact, and sturdy."

"I never thought of it that way," she said, "but you are quite right."

"And yet, that simple plan is actually a product of a succession of accidents and experiments that—"

"Somehow blend into a single, harmonious whole."

"Yes," the earl said and gave her a quizzical look. "Yes, that's exactly it, Miss Fairbanks."

"Oh, please call me Hannah. Miss Fairbanks makes me sound like an old spinster."

"But I thought that was your dearest ambition, to be an old spinster."

She gave an involuntary little chirp, then burst into outright laughter. The man was a charlatan. He had everyone fooled into believing him a starchy aristocrat, yet he was as big a tease as his brother. "Maybe so," she said at last, "but I'm not there yet! So, please call me Hannah. At least until such time as you may rightfully refer to me as the elderly Miss Fairbanks."

"As you wish, Hannah," he said. A slight twist of his mouth registered his honest distaste for such informality.

"Do not worry, my lord," she said. "I shall not next be asking to address you as Miles." She blanched at the very idea. This man would never be anything other than *my lord* so far as she was concerned. "That would not be right at all. You are an earl, and—"

"Elderly?"

She laughed again. "No! But you outrank me by

more degrees than I can count. And you are my host. It wouldn't be right. Besides, Lottie would have my hide. Does she call you Miles?"

"Not yet."

"And neither shall I. And so, my lord, please tell me more about how parts of the original house came to be incorporated into the current structure."

They strolled on together, stopping frequently so the earl could explain the history of each section of the house. Hannah was impressed with the depth of his knowledge. But then, it was his house, and so he ought to know its history. But Hannah suspected that not many estate owners knew their houses half as well.

They stood for some time before the south front while the earl explained that it was the only completed wing of Jones's original design. He spoke of the Italian influences as well as that of the French architect de Caus. He spoke of the formal gardens that had once fronted this wing. He spoke lovingly of each dormer and balustrade, each molding and bay.

"You really love it, don't you?" Hannah interrupted without thinking.

The earl turned and smiled down at her. "It's not often I have such an attentive audience to my lectures," he said. "I am sorry to have rambled on so. But yes, I do love it. I am bound to Epping by ties that stretch back farther than memory. But I am bound by inclination as well. I am not ashamed to admit it is my favorite place in the world. I love it all. Not just the hall, but the gardens, the grounds, the forests, the river, the pastures, the sheep, the coverts, the hedgerows, the village, St. Bidd's—everything."

He looked about him as he spoke with a gaze that seemed to drink it all in as though he could never get enough of it. "If I didn't feel honor-bound to do my duty at Lord's once a year, I'd never leave here."

He stiffened suddenly, as if recollecting himself.

Hannah got the distinct impression he had not meant to say so much to her. All at once the friendly openness was gone, and the aristocratic reserve was firmly back in place.

"What a selfish host I am," he said. "I am neglecting my other guests." He nodded in the direction of the rest of the party, who had long ago strolled on past them to the parterre gardens. "Perhaps we can continue our conversation another time, Hannah. Shall we join the others in the garden?"

Hannah wanted to say, "No, let's not." But for once she kept her tongue between her teeth.

They walked in silence, but he became the amiable host once again as soon as they reached the others. He lost no time in reclaiming Charlotte's attention, which, of course, took little effort at all.

Hannah kept herself slightly behind the others so she could easily observe Lord Strickland and Charlotte. Her sister tapped his arm flirtatiously, and he leaned in close to hear what she had to say. Though the earl's expression remained sober, Charlotte flashed him a dazzling smile. Was he teasing her sister as he had teased Hannah? She could not be certain from this angle and distance, but she could swear his eyes had lost their twinkle.

Hannah heaved a sigh and shuffled along the gravel path, kicking at a stone with the surprisingly unscuffed toe of her new kid half boot. She supposed she must get used to the idea of having the earl as a brother-in-law. He was a perfectly decent man and a vast improvement over Charlotte's first husband, who had been a pompous bore. She ought to have been pleased for her sister.

Why, then, could she not shake the notion that, despite his wealth and rank and good looks, he was ill-suited to Charlotte?

And, more important, why did she presume to think it was any of her business?

"You must know, my love, that I have only the best intentions. It is not for myself that I do this, but for our daughters. They need a mother."

Miles stood in the fading afternoon light in the Lady Chapel at St. Biddulph's, in front of the tomb of the late Countess of Strickland, his wife. He came here several days each week, at times when he knew the church would be empty, to speak to Amelia—to give her the news of the day, to tell her of the latest antics and accomplishments of their children, to share his troubles. He spoke to her in death just as he had done in life.

"I need you to understand, Amelia, to believe me when I say that you can never be replaced in my heart. But if you could see the girls . . . little Caro. You would not believe how she chatters and chatters, and she's just gone three. But she's so open and trusting and fearless. I'm afraid she will need a guiding hand to keep her safe. I do what I can, of course, but she . . . she needs a mother.

"And Amy. Poor little Amy. She's just the opposite of Caro. She's all closed up and scared. Afraid to love anyone lest they be taken away as . . . as you were. She keeps her distance by being cross and sullen and quiet. And she clings to me like a lifeline. Sometimes at night when I tuck her in and give her a hug, she cries and holds on to me and won't let go. So I hold her until she falls asleep.

"I'm afraid for her sometimes. Afraid she'll never learn to trust, to love. My dear Amelia, our daughter is so fragile, she needs a mother so badly. . . ."

He stopped and rubbed the bridge of his nose, trying to ease the stab of pain between his eyes. After a few deep breaths, he reached out and ran a finger along the letters of her name carved deep into the marble.

"Oh, God. Why do I feel like I am betraying you? Why do I sometimes feel sick to my stomach over the whole thing? If it was just for me, for my sake, I don't think I would ever marry again. I had everything I ever wanted with you, my love. You know that. I can't replace you. I don't want to replace you. But, dammit, I have to. I have to."

He pushed away from the tomb and began to pace the width of the tiny chapel. The click of his boot heels upon the uneven ancient tiles echoed loudly as he walked.

"It's not as though I was in love with her. I hardly know her. And she's different from you, Amelia. Or maybe it's just different courting a more mature woman, I don't know. And I'm older, too. God, it feels strange. I never thought to be going through this again, you know, this business of courtship. It's been so long, I'm not sure I even know what to do."

He gave a self-conscious laugh. "But she does, by God. Do you think she knows how obvious she is? Or does it even matter? We both know what is going on. And she is attracted to me, that much is clear. I will not lie to you, Amelia, and pretend that it doesn't please me. I suppose I am flattered by her attraction.

"But in the end, I am just a man, my dear, and weak. Despite everything, I cannot help responding to her. I am intrigued by her."

He stopped pacing and sat down heavily on one of the narrow wooden benches in the chapel.

"Do you hate me for that? Can you forgive me?"

He tilted his head back and watched the fading light through the tracery window. A last weak beam of sunlight fell eerily upon one of the other occupants of the chapel—a carved effigy of a knight in chain mail and surcoat, purported to represent Sir John de Montrenaux, a distant ancestor to Miles and patron of much of the thirteenth-century rebuilding at St. Biddulph's. Miles had always liked to believe that Sir John held guard over Amelia and the other chapel occupants, his fierce countenance and long sword warding off all offenders.

He turned from his contemplation of the effigy, the stone darkened and the carving worn almost smooth with the years, to face the pristine marble of his wife's tomb.

"She really is everything I have wanted in a wife," he continued, "if I can't have you back. Aside from her age and circumstances, which make her particularly suitable, she has charm, confidence, wit.

"And she is very beautiful, of course. Not in the way that you were, my love. She doesn't have your yellow-gold hair or your fine, translucent complexion."

Miles had been struck by Amelia's fragile beauty the first time he'd laid eyes on her at Lady Crutchley's ball. But as he tried to conjure up an image of that beauty just now, only a general impression came to mind. Good Lord, it had been just over two years and he was already forgetting the details of her face. How was that possible?

He dropped his head into his hands, so shamed by such an unconscionable lapse that he was unable even to look at the carved letters of her name. Thank God he still had her portrait in the Long Gallery and the miniature he kept in his bedchamber. He closed his eyes and concentrated on the portrait, the flat, frozen, two-dimensional image, and soon found that his memories still had the power to breathe life into that likeness. He had not forgotten, after all.

He looked up, sighed, and resumed his description of Lady Abingdon.

"She doesn't have your deep blue eyes or brows that turn up at the ends. She doesn't have that smile that transformed your whole face and crinkled up your eyes. Amy has your smile, by the way. Did you know? Her eyes crinkle up just as yours did, though less often, I am sorry to say.

"But she smiled yesterday. Did I tell you? She did more than smile, she actually giggled. I hadn't heard her laugh in so long that I almost lost my composure in front of my guests."

His chest seized up at the memory of his daughter's flushed cheeks and shy laughter. He would lose his composure here in the church if he was not careful. "It is the damnedest thing," he said. "Lady Abingdon's younger half sister is with her, you see. Miss Fairbanks. She is the most delightful girl. You would like her, Amelia. She is thoroughly unaffected and ingenuous. She just blurts out whatever is on her mind.

"She is almost twenty and hasn't yet had a Season due to her mother's illness and death. She claims no interest in ever having a Season in Town. She says she hopes she will never be married, but I suspect she will not get her wish. She has these enormous blue eyes, you see. Someday some man is going to find those eyes irresistible.

"Lady Abingdon wants to bring her out in the spring, but Miss Fairbanks is hoping for another relation to cock up his toes so she can go back into mourning and skip the whole thing. Ha!

"I swear that girl comes close to stripping me of all my patrician dignity. How she does make me laugh!"

Even now he found himself chuckling aloud at the thought of the outspoken young girl with her wayward curls and dimpled smile.

And rather shapely ankles.

He started. Where had that inappropriate image come from? The recollection of Hannah on the floor with the children, her skirts hiked up halfway to her knees?

He would not tell Amelia about the ankles.

"Which reminds me of my original point," he continued, dragging his thoughts back to the issue at hand, "that Miss Fairbanks is responsible for Amy's giggles. She has a way with children. I confess that when I first met her, I wondered if she wasn't still in the schoolroom herself. She has these dimples, you see. Anyway, the children adore her. I found Caro climbing all over her in the nursery, squealing with delight. And then I watched in absolute astonishment as Amy crawled onto her lap and giggled.

"When I tucked Amy in last night, she told me how much fun they had with Miss Fairbanks. Apparently she played all sorts of games with them and told them stories. Amy asked if she would be staying long. Her little chin began to quiver when I told her Miss Fairbanks would only be here for the month."

Miles had wanted to tell Amy that if Miss Fairbanks wished it she could stay forever, he was that grateful to the girl.

"Perhaps if I marry Lady Abingdon," he continued, "we can have Miss Fairbanks come to stay with us until she marries. The girls would love that, although I am not so sure how Lady Abingdon would feel about it."

A tiny shadow crossed the window and came to a stop on the external tracery. A linnet? He hoped so, and hoped the little bird's song would reach inside the chapel. Amelia had loved the linnets that nested in the trees around Epping. Perhaps this one would sing for her now.

Miles rose from the bench and straightened his coattails. He walked up to the tomb and laid both hands upon its cool marble.

"It is getting dark, my love, and I must return to the hall. I will visit you again soon. I love you. Never doubt that. Whatever happens with Lady Abingdon, know that I will always love you."

He left the chapel and walked through the presbytery and down the nave. He stopped briefly beneath one of the round nave arches and gazed up at the double rows of *voussoirs*. It had been a long time since he had taken note of the thin Roman bricks that composed the double rings above each arch. What sort of building had those bricks originally adorned before his Saxon ancestors had used them here?

Miss Fairbanks—Hannah—was right. The old church really was quite special.

Chapter 6

"What are all those other buildings?" Amy asked, one chubby finger pointing at a drawing in the sketchbook Hannah balanced on her lap. While the twins frolicked at the lake's edge with tiny Caro, the earl's solemn eldest daughter had not left Hannah's side. For some inexplicable reason, the little girl had developed a fierce attachment to Hannah and had begun to follow her around like a lost puppy.

All the family and guests at Epping had taken advantage of the unusually warm weather and gathered for a picnic at the edge of the ornamental lake. After the meal most of the others had wandered off in various directions, exploring the grounds around the lake. The earl and Charlotte had walked together in the direction of a nearby copse.

Hannah had not wanted to join any of the other adults. Watching her sister with the earl had put her in an oddly peevish mood. She decided she preferred the company of the children. She had grown weary of the courtship rituals taking place around her: the well-choreographed, elegant country dance of Charlotte and the earl, and the skittish movements of Miss Wetherby and the major. Both couples were being perfectly foolish, as far as Hannah was concerned. She had no patience with all the dissimulation and hypocrisy of Society's prescribed rituals. She would get more sensible conversation out of the children.

With the earl's permission, Hannah had dismissed Miss Barton, the twins' governess, for the afternoon, and Mrs. Lindquist, the girls' nurse, and had volunteered to entertain the children.

After a boisterous game of blindman's buff, she was pleased to relax with Amy beneath the shade of an ancient elm. Hannah had spent another fascinating morning at St. Biddulph's—studying the intact Saxon portions of the structure—and so when asked to sketch something, the old church was the first thing to come to mind. She had decided to sketch it as it might have appeared when first constructed toward the end of the seventh century.

"Those are just imaginary buildings," Hannah replied. "The church is quite old, you see, and when it was new, it was probably surrounded by other buildings like these. It was part of a monastic settlement—sort of like an abbey."

The twins bounded up the bank at that moment and plopped down on the blanket next to Amy. Caro toddled close behind.

"What a abbey?" Amy asked.

"That's where monks live," her cousin Henry replied, with all the self-satisfied condescension of an eight-year-old boy for a five-year-old girl.

"What a monk?" Amy asked, undaunted by male superiority.

Henry was not so quick with an answer this time and looked imploringly at Hannah. She let him squirm for a moment, as though waiting for him to answer. Finally, she smiled and said, "Monks are holy men who devote their lives to God and the Church."

"I saw a picture of a monk once," Charlie announced. "He wore robes and had funny hair."

"That's right," Hannah said. "Something like this." She quickly sketched a plump, tonsured monk with a gap-toothed grin, eliciting peals of laughter from the children.

"What happened to all those other buildings?" Henry asked. "The ones round the church?"

"They were destroyed by Danish invaders," she replied.

"Destroyed?" the twins exclaimed in unison.

"Didn't the English fight back?" Henry asked.

"I am sure they did," Hannah replied. "But remember, this was a religious settlement and probably not prepared for invasion and battle. There may not have been a stronghold or fortress nearby to protect it."

"But what about Epping Hall?" Amy asked. "The people here would have helped."

"Of course they would have, my dear," Hannah replied and ruffled the girl's soft blond curls. "But Epping Hall was not here yet."

"Not here?" Amy said, eyes wide with disbelief. "But I thought it was always here."

Hannah laughed. "Perhaps it has been," she said, "in one form or another." She recalled the earl's words comparing the hall's design to a medieval keep. "Before the present hall was built, perhaps an older building—a castle, even—stood on this spot. Let me see. What might it have looked like?"

While all four children crowded around to watch, Hannah turned to a fresh page in the sketchbook and quickly outlined a fairy tale castle with battlements and turrets, portcullis and moat. In the window of one fanciful turret she drew two girls with long, braided hair, one fair and one dark, dressed in flowing gowns and pointed headdresses. At the base of the turret she drew two knights in armor, broadswords held high.

"And here are two damsels in distress," Hannah said, "Lady Amelia and Lady Caroline, being rescued by the brave and strong Sir Charles and Sir Henry."

With that, the boys were up, sticks in hand, ready to

do battle. Hannah put an arm around each little girl and feigned terror. "Save us, good knights. Save us!"

"What are they saving us from?" asked the pragmatic Amy.

"A dragon!" Henry announced. "Here is the evil fire-breathing dragon," he said and pointed to the earl's mastiff, Bounder, who lay just beyond the elm's shade, basking in the afternoon sun. "Up, you monster, and we will fight you to the death!"

Bounder lifted one eyelid, offered an indifferent look in the direction of the boy waving a stick at him, yawned, and dropped his head back onto his paws. Clearly, the old dog was having none of it.

"He's no good as a dragon," Charlie said.

"But we *need* a dragon," Henry said.

Hannah rose to her knees and snarled. "I am the evil dragon!" she proclaimed. "And if you do not catch me, I will eat your fair cousins!"

The girls squealed with delight as Hannah pretended to bite them. The twins came at her with sticks and soon were chasing her round and round the tree. Hannah scampered up onto one of the low branches and growled at the boys from above.

"Down, evil dragon! Down!"

"Hannah!"

The familiar shriek of her sister distracted Hannah and caused her to lose her footing. Before she knew what had happened, she found herself sprawled on the ground at the base of the tree, staring into a pair of gleaming top boots.

The children collapsed with laughter. Hannah groaned and dropped her head into her hands. Hang it all, now there would be the devil to pay. Charlotte was hissing her displeasure already.

"How dare you behave so disgracefully?" Her sister kept her voice low, though her tone was laced with steel. If the earl hadn't been there, she probably would have shouted. "You are a young lady, not some wild savage."

The last words were spit out with such venom that Hannah almost cowered.

"Miss Fairbanks? Are you unharmed?"

Hannah lifted her face to find the earl, in all his pristine aristocratic elegance, still standing before her. He looked down at her, his brow furrowed as though concerned, ever the solicitous host. And yet his dark eyes betrayed the merest glimmer of amusement.

"I am quite well, my lord," Hannah replied, unable to completely suppress the grin that tugged at the corners of her mouth.

"Then please," Charlotte said in a chilly undertone, "get up and tidy yourself. You look a fright."

The earl reached out a gloved hand to assist her, his eyes completely sober now. Hannah sighed. There was almost no graceful way in which to rise from her awkward position. She was sure to incur a further measure of Charlotte's disapproval, yet there was nothing for it but to allow herself to be hauled to her feet.

She placed her hand in the earl's. The sun-warmed kid of his glove enveloped her fingers. After ensuring he had a good grip—a seemingly endless moment during which Hannah forgot to breathe—Lord Strickland tugged her upward.

Her feet, predictably, got all tangled up in her skirts, and she lost her balance. If the earl hadn't held on tightly to her hand and steadied her with another hand at her elbow, she would have surely fallen flat on her face—again.

Charlotte gave a disparaging cluck, the children continued to giggle, all the while Hannah stared up into the earl's brown eyes. Suddenly, and for perhaps the first time in her life, she heard the oft-repeated words of Charlotte's frequent scolds echoing in her head, and knew them to be true. It was as if a heavy fog had dissipated in the sunlight, and all at once she could see with perfect clarity. Charlotte was right. She had been right all along.

Despite a mature intelligence in certain academic areas, Hannah saw that her behavior at times—at most times—was willful and childish.

Though it had never mattered to her before, as she stood mere inches from the earl, their gazes locked, and his hand still clasping hers, she felt thoroughly ashamed of her hoydenish behavior.

Hannah's cheeks flushed with embarrassment as she plucked dried leaves from her hair. She was unable to meet anyone's eyes, even those of the tittering children, who danced about her rumpled and grass-stained skirts.

Why couldn't she be more like Charlotte? Poised and elegant. Adult.

The twins chattered loudly about dragons, but Hannah paid little attention. When Charlotte whispered something about changing into clean clothes, Hannah turned without a word and followed her sister back to the hall.

"She didn't do anything wrong," Amy said, scowling at the retreating forms of Hannah and Charlotte. "You leave her alone!" she shouted.

"Amy!" Miles took his eldest daughter firmly by the shoulders. "You are not to be rude to our guests."

"I don't care. She's mean and I don't like her." Amy thrust out her lower lip in the petulant manner that had become so familiar during the past two years. The giggles Miles had been so pleased to hear a few moments earlier had been replaced by Amy's more customary sullenness.

He cast a glance in the direction of the two women and hoped to God Charlotte had not heard Amy's outburst. She gave no indication of having heard, appear-

ing to be involved in an intense conversation with
Hannah. Or, more precisely, she appeared to be lectur-
ing, not conversing. Hannah looked straight ahead as
she walked and did not appear to be participating in
any way. No doubt she was receiving a sound scolding
from her sister.

The notion of scolding recalled his attention to Amy.
She stood glaring up at him, pouting. He scooped her
up into his arms and walked toward the lake's edge.
"We need to have a little talk, you and I," he said.
Though she normally clung to him at every opportunity, Amy seemed to know he was unhappy with her
and wriggled to be put down. He obliged her and
watched as she busied herself among the reeds and
grasses, searching for pebbles to toss in the water.

Miles bent and picked up a handful of stones, se-
lected a round, flat one, and skimmed it across the
lake. Four bounces. A middling performance for one
who had, years ago, been capable of seven as easily as
snapping his fingers. He was out of practice.

"Amy, why do you not like Lady Abingdon?"

With an elaborate overhand toss, she flung a pebble
into the lake. "She's mean and she doesn't like Hannah. Hannah is my friend."

"Oh, I think you're wrong, sweetheart. She is Hannah's big sister and looks out for her. I am sure she
loves her as much as you love Caro."

Amy gave a very expressive little snort. Where on
earth had she picked that up? He would have to have
a chat with Mrs. Lindquist.

"And besides," he continued, "she is our guest here
at Epping. We must all treat her with kindness and
courtesy. I can only hope she did not hear your very
unkind words a few moments ago. I would hate for
her to think my daughters are in the habit of behaving
rudely toward guests."

"But, Papa—"

"You must promise me that from now on you will treat Lady Abingdon with as much courtesy as you treat Hannah."

"But, Papa, I can't help it. She's not like Hannah. I don't like her. I don't want her to be my mama."

Miles froze in mid-throw, then tossed the stone absently in the water. He bent down on his haunches, turned Amy toward him, and stroked her soft cheek with his thumb. "What makes you think Lady Abingdon is going to be your mama?" he asked.

Amy gave a tiny shrug, but looked him straight in the eye. "I heard Lindy talking to Miss Barton. They said you was maybe going to marry Lady Ab . . . Lady Abi . . . that lady. Are you, Papa?"

Good Lord. He wasn't quite ready to have this conversation. When he had that chat with Mrs. Lindquist, he really must caution her against such indiscreet remarks.

"I don't know, poppet," he said at last. "Wouldn't you like to have a new mama someday?"

Amy hunched a shoulder, then turned away and played at sorting pebbles.

"Amy, you know, don't you, that no one can ever replace your real mama? Not for you and not for me, either. We will always love her, even though she has gone away forever. But sometimes . . . sometimes you get the chance to have a second mama. Someone who will love you and guide you and help you and Caro grow up into fine young ladies. Wouldn't you like that, poppet?"

"You mean she would be like a teacher?"

"Not exactly. You will have a real teacher, a governess like Miss Barton, in a few more years. But a mama is different. A new mama would teach you other things, important things to help you grow up to be a good person. She would be there, just as I am, to talk to you, to help you understand things. I do my best, Amy, but I am only a papa. Sometimes a little girl needs a mama."

"Hannah teaches us things."

Miles sighed. He didn't know if she was understanding any of this. "Does she?"

"Yes. Wait, I'll show you." Amy scurried up the bank to the base of the elm tree where Hannah had been so precariously perched when he and Charlotte had come upon them earlier. Miles took the opportunity to stretch his legs, which had become cramped from his crouching position. Amy returned within a moment, however, carrying a large sketchbook. Caro, apparently bored with the antics of her older cousins, who still played at knights, tagged along behind her sister.

Amy opened the sketchbook and held it out to Miles. He crouched down again so they could all look at it together. It was open to a picture of St. Biddulph's, beautifully drawn in meticulous detail.

"See these buildings?" Amy asked, pointing to the low structures flanking the church. "Hannah says they were there a long time ago. They were part of a . . . a . . . " Her face screwed up in thought as she tried to remember the word. "An abbey!" she said triumphantly.

"That's right," Miles said, beaming with pride at his beautiful, clever girl.

"And holy men lived there, like this one." Amy pointed to a funny little sketch of a rotund, grinning monk. She told him in awed tones about how the abbey had been destroyed a long time ago by bad men. And about how Epping had been a castle where knights had fought the bad men, and dragons, too.

Hannah's fanciful drawing of the castle was charming. When he heard the tale of the ladies in distress and the knights who came to their rescue, of the reluctant dragon, Bounder, he laughed along with his daughters. He could not recall when he'd seen Amy so animated, so happy. *Bless you, Hannah Fairbanks.*

"We like Hannah, Papa," Amy said. "She's fun and teaches us things. Why can't she be our new mama?"

Hannah?

Good Lord, he ought to have seen this coming. Hannah, for God's sake.

He must handle this situation with care. Somehow, Amy had to get this ridiculous idea out of her head. He hadn't yet made up his mind about Charlotte, but there was certainly no possibility in the world of his marrying Hannah. She was about as far from the sort of wife he wanted as she could be. Hannah as the Countess of Strickland? He almost laughed out loud.

"Hannah cannot be your new mama, poppet, because I am not going to marry her. She's much too young to be your mama. But I am sure she will always be your friend."

"Will we have to have that other lady for our mama, then?" Amy asked, an obstinate look in her eye.

"I don't know," Miles replied.

And he didn't. It concerned him that Amy did not like Charlotte, but Amy could be contrary at the best of times. It was true, though, that Charlotte had not warmed to his daughters as he had hoped. She was awkward with them; but she had no children of her own and had likely not been much around children. Perhaps she just needed more time with them, time to become accustomed to them.

She certainly had no trouble warming to Miles. When they were quite alone and unobserved among the trees, she had let him kiss her. Invited him to kiss her, in fact, with her rather open flirtation. He could not have avoided that kiss, even had he wanted to, without appearing to insult her. It had been pleasant, if not passionate. He suspected she would have allowed more—much more—but he did not want to give any false impressions when he was still ambivalent about the situation.

"I don't know," he repeated. "Even so, I expect you both to be polite and courteous to Lady Abingdon while she is here at Epping. Is that clear?"

Amy gave another snort—where *had* she learned such a thing? Miles wondered—and trudged back up the bank to join the twins.

"I t'ink she's pretty."

"Who, Caro?"

"The lady."

"Lady Abingdon?"

Caro nodded, and Miles lifted her up into his arms and kissed her cheek. "Yes, she is, pumpkin. She certainly is."

Oh, why couldn't Amy be more like Caro, who took to everyone with such ease? But then, she had not been so hurt as Amy by her mother's death. She had been only an infant when Amelia died.

Miles was more convinced than ever that poor little Amy, so moody and temperamental, needed a mother's hand to lead her out of her sulky nature.

Was Charlotte the one to do it? She may not have had experience with young children, but she had been responsible for Hannah. Her experience with her own headstrong younger sister could serve as good practice for taming Amy.

But then Hannah, much to his reluctant delight, had not yet been tamed.

Chapter 7

"I have tried and tried, but I don't know what more I can say to you." Charlotte sank into a wing chair next to the fireplace and looked thoroughly cast down.

Hannah felt sick. Her stomach roiled with tension and nerves and guilt. Genuinely ashamed of her behavior, of her thoughtless determination not to be a lady, she was sorry to have caused her sister such distress. Truly sorry.

And yet, what troubled her most, what set her head to spinning so that she was positively dizzy, were persistent images of the earl when he had helped her to her feet. The expertly polished top boots without a speck of dirt upon them. The touch of his hand. The close-fitting buckskin breeches. The twinkle in his eye. The perfectly tailored bottle green frock coat.

If all gentlemen in Society were turned out in such easy elegance, Charlotte was right. Hannah would never take. Such a man would never be interested in a rumpled, dirty hoyden with leaves in her hair.

Not that she cared. She had never intended to fall in with Charlotte's plans for a Season in Town. Courtship and marriage had never been important to her. The thought rankled, that was all—the realization that a man like the earl could never be interested in her.

A man like the earl? Good heavens, what was she doing? She had no business thinking of Lord Strickland in such a way. He was Charlotte's project and none of Hannah's concern.

Except that a match between him and Charlotte was bound to be a disaster.

"Are you listening at all, Hannah?"

Hannah sat curled on the windowseat of her bedchamber, knees tucked up under her chin. It was no way for a lady to sit, she supposed. With a weary sigh, she straightened her legs and swung them over the edge of the seat. She folded her hands in her lap and looked up at Charlotte.

Frustration marked her sister's face, a deep frown lining her perfect brow.

Yes, Hannah had listened. She had heard every word about the impropriety of a young woman romping and running and tree-climbing with the children as if she were one of them. About her shameful appearance before their noble host, with her hair falling about her shoulders and her skirts stained and torn. About the dirt on her face and the leaves in her hair.

Yes, she had heard it all. Was that how Lord Strickland saw her, as a scruffy, cloddish adolescent? Had she misinterpreted that twinkle in his eye? Had he been laughing at her?

Her cheeks burned with shame, and for a moment she thought she might actually cry. "I'm listening, Lottie," Hannah said at last.

"Good," Charlotte said. "I do not wish to speak ill of the dead. Your mother was a sweet and gentle woman, but she gave you far too much rein. It is more than just climbing trees and cavorting on the nursery floor like an infant. You are impossibly forthright in both speech and expression. Did your mother never teach you to school your features, to mask your feelings, to employ a bit of tact before you are completely ruined socially by some unforgivable gaffe?"

Charlotte did not appear to expect an answer, knowing full well Hannah's mother had never tried to force her into a socially acceptable mold.

"Last evening at supper, for example," she went on. "Was it really necessary to mention Mr. Rooke's corsets?"

The local squire and his wife had been invited to join them for supper. The rotund Mr. Rooke, whose waistcoat had threatened to pop its buttons throughout the evening, had been seated next to Hannah. He was a very gregarious and animated gentleman. He used his whole body when he spoke, lending emphasis to each word with some movement or gesture. The sound of his corset punctuated every move.

"All that creaking and snapping," Hannah said, "was enough to drive anyone to the brink. I merely asked him to speak up so I could hear him above his corsets."

Charlotte shook her head and clicked her tongue.

"He did not seem insulted," Hannah went on, defensively. "He laughed."

"It was indelicate of you to have mentioned it at all," Charlotte said. "The poor man was scarlet with embarrassment."

"How could you tell? He was scarlet all evening, he was so tightly laced. I was afraid he might have an apoplexy on the spot."

"Hannah . . . "

Charlotte's face puckered with a look of pure frustration. *Blast!* She was right. Hannah was a loose-tongued, awkward, insensitive dolt.

"I'm sorry, Lottie. Truly I am. And I'm sorry I embarrassed you in front of the earl today. Have I ruined it for you, do you think?"

Charlotte glared at her in silence for a moment, then her expression relaxed, and she settled back more deeply in the chair. "I don't know," she said. "I don't think so. I hope not." She gave a wan little half smile, and for a moment she looked as though she were a thousand miles away, lost in her thoughts. "We were . . . we were making headway, I believe."

The look in Charlotte's eye made Hannah shudder. Hang it all, had the man been making love to her already? She began to feel more queasy and clutched at her stomach.

"Do you . . . do you expect an offer, then?"

Charlotte's gaze came back to meet Hannah's. She gave an arrogant little shrug. "One should never *expect* such a thing, my dear. But one should always be prepared."

"Prepared to accept, you mean?"

Charlotte gave her a look of disbelief, then began to laugh. "Would *you* reject an offer from such a man?"

"I am unlikely to receive one," Hannah replied.

"True. But the point is, what woman alive would reject an offer from the Earl of Strickland? This beautiful estate, his fortune, his lineage, his exquisite manners, his good looks. The man is nearly perfect. Oh, I suppose I could wish for a bit more . . . more ardor, though I imagine one should not expect it from a man of such scrupulous dignity."

Aha! Perhaps he had not in fact been making love to Charlotte every time she dragged him off alone.

"But I don't mind telling you, Hannah," she continued, "this man is the catch of a lifetime."

"And my antics are hampering your courtship."

Charlotte did not reply, but her shrug was sufficiently eloquent.

"I *am* sorry, Lottie. I never meant to cause you such trouble, and after all you've done for me. I will try to do better, I promise."

Charlotte smiled. "Thank you, my dear. That is all I can ask. I only want us both to make a good impression, you know. The Epping ball is next week. It will be a good opportunity for each of us to shine. You look so pretty when you dress up, Hannah. If you will only make an effort to watch your tongue, and your feet, I will be very pleased with you."

"I will try," Hannah said. She owed as much to Charlotte. Despite her own feelings on a match between her sister and Lord Strickland, it was what Charlotte wanted. Hannah had no right to interfere. If Charlotte wanted this man, she would likely have him, regardless of Hannah's behavior. Even so, Hannah owed her sister more respect and support. The best way to do this, she decided, was to stay out of sight as much as possible.

Over the next few days, Hannah spent more and more time at St. Biddulph's. She became so absorbed in her explorations that thoughts of Charlotte and the earl seldom plagued her. She was much more interested in the sunken ambulatory and the possibility that it might have once surrounded a late Saxon crypt.

Mr. Cushing allowed her to roam freely about the church, but insisted she have tea with him each day and tell him of her discoveries. They engaged in lively debates on the dating of the chancel arch and the possibility of a crypt beneath the apse.

When an excursion to the nearby market town of Oundle was suggested by Mr. Wetherby, Hannah declined the invitation, preferring to spend another day at St. Biddulph's. She was not excited, as was Charlotte, by Cousin Winifred's stories of Oundle's bobbin lace industry. Shopping for fripperies was low on Hannah's list of favorite activities.

But when all the others tried to persuade her to come along, a speaking glance from Charlotte was all she needed to remind her of her promise to behave like a lady. A lady would graciously accept the invitation and make a show of enjoying herself.

And so Hannah agreed to go.

Major Prescott pulled her aside as they waited for

the carriages in the inner courtyard. "I know you'd rather poke around old buildings than go shopping with the other ladies," he said. "Did you know that Fotheringay Castle was near Oundle?"

"Where poor Mary Queen of Scots was executed?"

"The very place."

"But it was long ago torn down, was it not?"

"So it was," the major said. "But did you know there's an inn at Oundle, the Talbot, that was built from the stones of Fotheringay, and that its staircase actually came from the castle?"

"Truly?"

"Truly," said the earl, who had joined them. "The inn was built during the early part of the seventeenth century, as were many of the buildings in the town. But what may prove more interesting to you, Miss Fairbanks—"

"Hannah."

"—Hannah, is the church of St. Peter."

"Another musty old pile of stones," the major said.

"Not as old at St. Bidd's," the earl said.

"But just as musty."

"Is there really an old church at Oundle?" Hannah asked, ignoring the major's teasing and beginning to get excited.

"There is indeed," the earl said. "It was originally built in the twelfth century, as I recall, though very little of the original Norman structure remains. Not as provocative as St. Bidd's, but you might find it interesting."

Hannah's spirits rose considerably with the possibility of exploring a Norman church. She had become so wrapped up in the glories of St. Biddulph's, she had forgotten that there might be other churches nearby worth a visit.

She kept her excitement in check, reminding herself of the promise to Charlotte. A lady would not bounce

on the carriage seat in her enthusiasm. She rode with
Major Prescott, Miss Wetherby, and Mr. Wetherby. The
major teased and flirted throughout the six-mile drive,
but Hannah suspected Miss Wetherby no longer saw
her as a threat, if she ever had. She had actually smiled
at Hannah once, and looked remarkably pretty when
she did.

They soon reached Oundle, a town of attractive
brick buildings and gabled houses with mullioned
windows.

After visiting the old market cross, viewing the fa-
bled staircase at the Talbot Inn, examining yard after
yard of bobbin lace in the shops on High Street, and
stopping for luncheon at the White Lion, Hannah
began to despair of ever seeing the old church.

Fearing no one else would ever suggest it, she decided to take the matter into her own hands.

"I am going to have a look at St. Peter's," she announced as they exited the White Lion.

"Not alone, Hannah," Charlotte said. "You must
find someone to accompany you."

Cousin Godfrey declared his intention of remaining
at the White Lion and enjoying another mug of porter.
Major Prescott claimed to have promised Miss
Wetherby a stroll along the River Nene.

"Then you must come along with Cousin Winifred
and me," Charlotte said. "She tells me there are more
shops along the Market Place, and one I particularly
wish to see that specializes in lace caps. Come along,
dear."

Hannah groaned, but did not argue. "Yes, Charlotte," she said.

"I would be happy to accompany you to the church,
Miss Fairbanks."

She almost shouted with glee at the earl's offer, but
held her tongue and turned to gauge Charlotte's reaction. Though she'd behaved, or so she thought, rather

well over the last few days, Hannah could not be sure Charlotte would appreciate her going off alone with Lord Strickland. She was loathe to set up Charlotte's back once again, especially after they'd been rubbing along together so well. Though it was a sacrifice to miss the church, a *lady* would not argue.

But those lace caps must have beckoned loudly, for Charlotte merely nodded and said, "Thank you, my lord. I am sure Hannah would appreciate your escort. She does so enjoy old churches."

Hannah smiled appreciatively at her sister, then began the walk to St. Peter's at a brisk clip. Her pace caused Miles to chuckle softly to himself. She had probably been waiting all day for someone to suggest visiting the church, but there were too many other distractions to tempt the rest of the company. Now that she had her chance, he thought she might break into a run. "It is just down the road, Miss Fairbanks—"

"Hannah."

"—Hannah. It will still be there even should we decide on a leisurely stroll."

"But the day is more than half gone already," she said in a breathless voice, "and I wish to see everything."

"Yes," he said, "I can see how important this is to you. Even more exciting than Mary Queen of Scots's staircase."

"Ha! I'd wager a monkey—if I had it—that the staircase wasn't built until a good fifty years after the poor queen's death. Old Fotheringay never saw the likes of that Jacobean staircase. Besides, I'd rather see a real Norman church any day."

"I know you would, Hannah, which is why I was so surprised to see you almost forgo the pleasure just now. I suspect you've seen more lace than you ever cared to see."

"Haven't I just! I thank you, my lord, for rescuing me from the lace caps." She shook her head and then lowered her voice, muttering to herself. "I declare, this lady business can be a dead bore."

"Lady business?"

She slowed her pace almost to a halt and her eyes widened, as though she had not meant for him to hear. She sighed, rolled her eyes heavenward, and continued marching toward the church like a soldier on maneuvers. She cast him a sheepish grin over her shoulder. "I suppose now that I've blurted out my predicament, I should explain. You see, I promised Lottie—Charlotte, that is—I'd stop behaving like a hoyden and act like a lady."

The earl choked back laughter as they approached the porch of St. Peter's. He'd seen very little of Hannah since the incident by the lake, and when she joined them for meals, she spoke hardly a word. He'd missed her liveliness and guileless candor. Now he began to understand what had happened.

She must have been given one hell of a scolding, poor girl. And all because she'd gone out of her way to amuse the children. Because she'd been perched in a tree with a good deal of ankle showing. Because her heavy curls couldn't seem to hold a hairpin. Because she knew how to have fun, something he seemed to have forgotten over the last few years.

Hannah could probably best his pitiful four bounces with ease.

"You have done a good job of honoring that promise," he said. "You have been positively demure these last few days."

She stopped on the porch and looked up at him, blue eyes flashing. "I have, haven't I?"

"Indeed. And I suspect it has not been easy."

She frowned, her brows knit together so tightly,

deep furrows formed bet
insulted her? "Forgive me,

She cut him off with a ra
right," she said, still frown
come easily to me, I fear. But it
became a true lady. If such a thing

He sincerely hoped it was not. H
fine the way she was. Ever since she
of the carriage that first day, Miles
oughly charmed by her lack of guile, he
plain speaking, her artless enthusiasm—
ciety's preference for studied ennui.

Her casual disregard for what others migh
her was one of the things he secretly envied
Hannah. He did not like to think that she was
coerced into putting on a proper show for those w
opinions should not matter to her.

"Being a lady does not necessarily mean losing
yourself," Miles said. "Your energy and honesty and
curiosity are what make you who you are, Hannah.
Don't lose all that in an effort to be something else."

She shrugged her shoulders, looking almost bash-
ful. "You are very kind, my lord. But I rather think Lottie has the right of it. It is time I grew up. I am a burden
to her."

"Oh, I think you are wrong. How could you ever be
a burden to Lady Abingdon?"

"By being such an embarrassment that you won't
marry her, that's how."

Hannah clapped a hand over her mouth the instant
the words were spoken. A scarlet flush crept up her
face all the way to her ears.

Miles could have laughed out loud at this outra-
geous girl, if not for the implications of her words.
Charlotte was that determined to have him, was she?
He had known it, of course, but to realize again how

...d not sit well ...of them. It

...church.
...e," she
...on the

...not
...on-
...is-
...and
...se at first,
...me immersed in
...et all that had gone be-

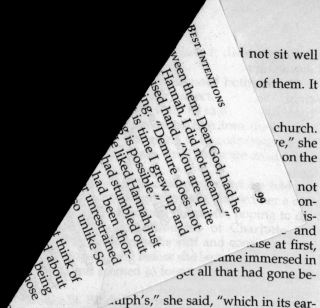

...lph's," she said, "which in its ear-
...ad aisles off the nave, the aisles in this
...are not original. The absence of bonding be-
...ween the nave and aisle walls is a clear indication.
However, this end of the nave—just here, you see?—
and much of the chancel is certainly twelfth century."

Miles found himself fascinated as she spoke at length and in considerable detail about the early masonry in the angles of the transepts, the corbels indicating the existence at one time of a central tower, the signs of a now-demolished staircase turret resulting in an uneven arcade. She amazed him, again, with the depth of her knowledge. He was completely swept away by her enthusiasm.

After an hour, Miles reluctantly announced that they must return to the White Lion and be on their way back to Epping Hall. Hannah's face crumpled in disappointment, but she said nothing and followed him down the nave. To revive her spirits, and to ensure the conversation had no possibility of returning to her earlier remark about Charlotte, Miles asked Hannah about her explorations at St. Biddulph's.

"I understand you spend several hours each day there," he said.

"Yes," she answered, but gave him a look that asked how he knew.

"I visit St. Bidd's fairly often myself," he said. He would not mention that his visits were primarily to converse with his dead wife. "Mr. Cushing has mentioned your work. You have certainly given the old man a new lease on life. I cannot recall when I last saw him so excited."

At his urging, Hannah spoke of her research and her theories. He was stunned and fascinated to discover she believed a Saxon crypt existed beneath the apse. He became so caught up in the discussion that he hadn't realized they'd reached the White Lion until he heard Charlotte say, "Here they are at last."

It was his turn to be disappointed, though he schooled his features in a way Hannah would have never been able to do. He had so enjoyed listening to her.

Not since his Oxford days had Miles encountered such scholarship. It was incredible, that the same young girl who fell out of trees and tripped over her tongue could lecture so knowledgeably on Saxon and Norman architecture. Yet she was equally radiant standing inside a church waxing poetic on quoining as she was tumbling on the nursery floor with his little girls.

What a charming paradox was Miss Hannah Fairbanks.

His eyes followed her up the steps of the White Lion. She turned and smiled at him, dimples winking. It wasn't until Lady Abingdon had casually brushed his arm that he realized he had not heard a single whispered word she'd spoken.

Chapter 8

"Tell me about Spain."

Rachel strolled next to George along the meandering bank of the River Nene. She did not take his arm, apparently determined to keep her distance. Her question took him off guard. He had not wanted to share that part of his life with her. She could never understand. No one who stayed safely back home in England could understand.

"Blazing sun and torrential rains," he said. "Mud and dust. Bad food. Boredom and battle."

"It changed you," she said.

"Yes." An understatement.

He caught her studying him, and she turned away. "Your skin is darker," she said, "your hair is lighter. You seem . . . broader a bit about the shoulders."

George looked down at himself and shrugged.

"You are different in other ways as well," she continued.

Indeed. "I was a boy when I left."

"And now—"

"And now I'd rather talk about something else." He stepped in front of her, stopped, and reached down to take both her hands in his. She resisted, but he held fast. They'd been circling each other like timid hedgehogs for the last few weeks. He was tired of it. He needed to understand where things stood.

"Why have you never married, Rachel? Is it . . . is it because of me, because of what happened?"

Rachel pulled her hands away and turned her back to him, staring out at the river. "I was wrong. You haven't changed at all. You still flirt with every female in sight, and you are still puffed up with your own consequence if you think my spinster state has anything to do with you."

Prickly as ever, hedgehog spines pointing outward, protecting her. He must coax her to uncurl. "Why, then?" he asked. "Surely you've had offers. Or is every man in the Midlands an idiot, or blind? You're a beautiful woman, Rachel."

He had moved to her side and saw, to his surprise, that she was blushing. An encouraging sign, he thought.

He would go on with his plan, say what he needed to say. She had been skittish and quiet since his return. But somehow, he must get her to talk about it. They must both face this thing between them.

"I have never stopped regretting what happened that night," he said. "Do you think you can ever find it in your heart to forgive me?"

She turned, and he searched her eyes, but she kept her expression closed, unreadable. Without a word, she wandered a bit ahead of him, away from the low riverbank toward a line of trees set along the beginning of the gentle rise leading into the center of Oundle. She did not speak for several excruciating minutes. She considered her reply. Resigned as an old soldier facing an enemy force ten times the size of his own, he prepared for her to tell him as politely as possible that there was no forgiveness for him.

"I forgave you a long time ago," she said at last. "But you left before I could tell you."

Dear God. Relief so powerful it left him weak caused

him to reach out a hand to steady himself against the trunk of a tree. Dear God, she had forgiven him.

All that time, and he had not known. Seven years. Seven years without a notion that she'd forgiven him. Would things have gone differently if he hadn't left? Would he even now be happily married to Rachel, living with their children on the small estate that had become his upon his majority?

But he had been young and hotheaded and unwilling to face up to his mistakes. Ever since he'd been a boy, he'd wanted to be a soldier. But his father had left each of his sons estates, in hopes they would all become gentlemen farmers, as Miles had done. But George had convinced Miles, distracted with his bride and set to leave for his wedding trip, to buy him the colors he'd always wanted.

He left Epping Hall, and Rachel, the next day and threw himself headlong into soldiering.

And all along, she had forgiven him.

"Ah, Rachel," he said. "I wish I'd known."

Her forgiveness acted as a sort of unexpected liberation. He rushed ahead like a private on quick march, words tumbling out in a compelling need to confess the whole.

"She meant nothing to me, you know," he said. "You never gave me a chance to explain."

"Please, I do not want—"

"It is just that I was young and green and arrogant as hell. She was older, sophisticated, and she made it very clear she wanted me. Nothing like that had ever happened to me before. Half the world here for Miles's wedding and women flirting like mad with the safe third son."

"George, don't—"

"And her. God, she was so blatantly available. She was the pursuer, Rachel. It wasn't me. I swear, she practically threw herself at me. I never set out to—"

"Please, George, I do not—"

"—hurt you. She was just so . . . so determined. And I was flattered and, God help me, willing. It was nothing to do with you, Rachel, or with us. It was just—"

"Stop!" Rachel's eyes were tightly shut and she had put her hands over her ears.

She did not want to hear more. But he was not finished.

George gently took her hands in his and moved them away from her ears. She would not look at him. "Rachel, I'm so sorry."

She lifted her head so sharply the brim of her bonnet almost clipped his chin. "The Hermitage," she said between clenched teeth. "You took her to the Hermitage."

"Oh, God." He had thought it was only Lady Deene—enough, certainly—but it had been the Hermitage all along. His and Rachel's favorite spot since they were children. And as they'd grown older and fallen in love, it had become a meeting place where they'd shared dreams and longings, and on one momentous occasion, much more.

When Lady Deene had made it clear she wanted him, Epping Hall was swarming with wedding guests. George couldn't take her to his own bedchamber, or hers. It was too dangerous, with guests and extra servants dashing all about.

And there had been the additional need for secrecy: Rachel mustn't find out.

So he had taken Lady Deene to the first and only place that came to mind—the thatched hut built by his grandfather as a rustic folly.

"How could you?" Rachel said, her voice tight with the anger he had fueled by dredging up the past. "How could you have taken her there?"

The awful thing was, he hadn't given a single thought to the implications of taking Lady Deene to the Hermitage. To his shame, he knew that if Rachel hadn't walked in on them, he would never have considered he'd violated anything sacred.

"That's the worst part, isn't it?" he said. "The place more than the act."

Her expression changed from anger to disappointment. She tugged her hands free and turned away from him. "It was our place," she said in a soft, sad voice. "I thought it was our place."

"And something so special has been forever ruined because you caught me there with Lady Deene."

"Another man's wife. And in the very place where you and I had . . ." Her voice caught. "It was more than I could bear, George."

Yes, he could see that now. He had not fully understood the depth of Rachel's anger at the time. He'd been contrite and guilt-ridden, but she hadn't budged. Young fool that he was, he'd called her stubborn and heartless.

"And so you, justifiably, lashed out at me, and I bolted." He leaned back against the tree and closed his eyes. "Rachel, Rachel. What a cad I was. How the devil could you possibly have forgiven me?"

"If you had stayed, I don't know if forgiveness would have come so easily. It would have been too hard to face you."

He opened his eyes to find her standing before him, pale and beautiful, protective hedgehog spines keeping him at bay. "And now?" he asked. "Is there still a chance for us, Rachel, after all this time?"

She looked away and he couldn't see beyond the brim of her bonnet, couldn't see her unreadable face. "To forgive is one thing," she said at last. "To forget is nearly impossible."

"I betrayed you, Rachel. I'm not likely to forget it, either. I've been punishing myself for seven years."

She whipped around to face him. "And what do you

expect now? That I should ignore what happened and fall into your arms?"

He smiled and stepped away from the tree. "The falling into my arms part would be nice. But I doubt either of us can ignore the past. I just need to know if it is an insurmountable obstacle. I still care for you, Rachel." He moved closer to her. She did not retreat. "I do not expect us to pick up where we left off. But I'd like to try and start all over. If you think there's a chance?"

A faint smile touched her lips. The hedgehog uncurled. "I suppose there's always a chance."

He reached out and took her hand again. When he was sure she wasn't going to pull away, he kissed her softly on the fingers. "That is more than I have a right to ask," he said. "Will you dance the opening set with me at the ball?"

"Yes. Yes, I think I'd like that."

Guests for the annual Epping ball, traditionally held to commemorate the completion of autumn threshing, began to arrive the day after the excursion to Oundle. Friends and neighbors throughout the Midlands descended upon the hall.

Miles, justly proud of his estate, showed off all his farming operations to those interested. While Winifred entertained the ladies back at the hall, Miles led an inspection of the farmlands. There was no shortage of farmers interested in his variation of Coke's four-course crop rotation, his modes of tillage, and his up-to-date tools and implements, including the very latest in threshing machines. It was due to those machines, introduced by his father some twenty years before and further improved in recent years, that allowed the annual ball, once a winter tradition, to be held earlier during the better weather of autumn.

"Threshing completed by Michaelmas." Joseph

Wetherby sat sprawled in an old leather chair in Miles's study. "What would our grandfathers have thought of all this modern technology?"

"I suspect they would wish they had had it," Miles replied. He stood by one of the sash windows in his study, overlooking the south lawn.

"Indeed," Joseph said. "With so much free time on their hands, they could have begun the hunt before November."

Joseph prattled on about the upcoming fox-hunting season and the quality of the grouse this year, but Miles paid little attention. Through the window, he watched as his daughters sat beneath one of the old beech trees with Hannah Fairbanks. He must remember to thank her for keeping his little girls distracted and away from the house during the frantic preparations for tomorrow's ball. They were not frolicking about, as was usual when he found them together, but were seated quietly, absorbed in a large picture book. Or perhaps it was Hannah's sketchbook, he could not tell.

He wished he had a sketchbook, not to mention the talent to use it. The scene he observed was worth capturing. Amidst the cultivated green lawns, the ancient beeches rose from smooth, gray-green trunks, their twisted limbs bending this way and that providing a perfect canopy of shade. The afternoon sun glinted off the soft golds and brilliant reds of their autumn foliage.

Against one thick centuries-old trunk sat Hannah in a bright yellow dress and his girls in white with pink sashes. Ah, what the much maligned Constable would do with such light and such colors.

"I say, Miles," Joseph said, jerking Miles's attention from the pastoral beauty out the window, "what do you make of this business with George and Rachel?"

Miles turned to face his friend, but remained half

perched on the deep windowsill. "I'm not certain," he said. "George hasn't confided in me. But it looks promising, don't you think?"

"I'd say they're both beginning to smell of April and May," Joseph replied. "And I confess, I'm glad for it. Although I cannot say that Rachel has actually pined for him all these years, she seems to have deliberately kept herself lonely. I suspect that though she may have convinced herself she hated him, she never got over his being her first true love."

"I'm afraid George deserved her scorn," Miles said. "He behaved abominably. He was cocky as hell, and that woman's interest only made him more so. Frankly, I think it was all for the best that he went into the army. It matured him. He's more self-assured but less cocky."

"Still charming as ever, though," Joseph said. "You ought to have heard him flirting like mad with that little Fairbanks chit on the way to Oundle."

Miles instinctively glanced out the window to the little chit in question. What the devil was George doing flirting with her?

"But Rachel got her share as well," Joseph continued. "I daresay the boy will always be able to charm the birds from the trees. Has he been sweet-talking your widow as well?"

Miles gave a derisive snort and continued to stare out the window.

"What's the matter, old chap? Has the Abingdon courtship hit a snag?"

Miles's first instinct was to close up; he did not particularly like to speak of such private matters. It made him uncomfortable. But this was Joseph.

"Really, Joe, it is more than a little disconcerting to attempt a courtship under such close scrutiny. At least in London one is surrounded by crowds. There is so much going on it can be assumed that all eyes in the room are not following one's every move. But here . . ."

"Here, unlike London, there are more opportunities to be alone with a lady."

"And greater expectations due to the number of such opportunities."

"Aha. Is the lady planning the bridal breakfast already, then?"

"Good God, I hope not. It's just so awkward having everyone acting as though the banns had been read."

"She's a beautiful woman, Miles. You could do worse."

"Do I detect a bit of interest on your own behalf?"

"No, by Jove, you do not. I merely make an observation." Joseph chuckled. "I confess, though, that if the lady were not so publicly meant for you, I might be tempted to indulge in a bit of dalliance."

Miles slapped the windowsill with the flat of his hand. "There, you see what I mean? Publicly meant for me, indeed. I tell you I feel quite out of control of this situation, as though I had no choice in the matter at all."

"Are you saying Lady Abingdon would not be your choice?"

"I don't know."

Those words seemed to have become Miles's watchwords of late. He did not know what he felt. He did not know what he wanted. He did not know what to do. He did not know.

All this confusion and uncertainty were utterly foreign to him. He was a man always in control. The only other time he could recall being so fuddled was when he'd met Amelia and been so top over tail in love he'd been unable to see straight. But he had no such excuse now. He certainly was not in love with Charlotte.

Perhaps that was the problem.

And yet, not so many weeks ago he had been perfectly clearheaded about the whole thing—few expectations, simple purpose, more than willing to fall in with Winifred's matchmaking scheme.

Miles could not pinpoint when it had all changed, when he had begun to feel as though a noose were tightening around his neck.

Joseph once again interrupted his thoughts. "I suppose that means we shall not be hearing any special announcements at tomorrow's ball?" he asked.

"Not unless you have one to make," Miles replied. "Dammit, Joe, I'm not ready."

"But I thought you wanted—"

"I don't know anymore." *Those words again.* "I'm sorry, old friend, I'm being dreadfully foolish, I fear. Charlotte is a beautiful, desirable woman who is, if I may be allowed to say so, obviously attracted to me. She would make a fine countess, I have no doubt."

"What are you afraid of?"

Miles stared at his friend's words. "Afraid?" Was he afraid? A very fine line separated fear and uncertainty. "Perhaps I'm only now realizing how big a decision this is."

"And you're afraid of making a mistake?"

"I suppose it comes down to that, does it not?" Miles said. "It would be a mistake I'd have to live with for the rest of my life. Oh, but I'm just jittery, old chap. It's utter foolishness. In the end, I will probably make her an offer. I simply need a bit more time, I believe."

"Well, I am looking forward to the ball in any case. I hope you will spare the beautiful widow for a dance with your oldest friend."

"With pleasure," Miles said. He smiled and imagined twirling about the room with Charlotte. She would no doubt look dazzling. He would open the ball with the most beautiful woman in the room. It made him proud to think of that, and of how all the other gentlemen would be jealous. So long as he kept his thoughts steered in that direction, he would be more at ease.

He must remember to reserve a set with Hannah as well. He suspected she would be a spirited dancer, she was so full of unbridled, youthful energy.

But oddly peaceful at the moment, he thought, as he shifted his position on the sill to watch the scene beneath the beech tree. The sight of Hannah with one of his daughters tucked snugly under each arm produced a queer feeling in his stomach. The three of them looked thoroughly comfortable and natural together.

Hannah said something that made all three of them laugh. Face flushed and dimpled, eyes dancing with some delight, she happened to look toward the window and caught Miles's eyes. She smiled, and he had the strangest inclination to crawl out the window and join them outside. Just for a moment, he experienced a most unnatural desire to curl up comfortably on her lap with his daughters and forget all about courtship and public expectations and private uncertainties.

But what the devil was he doing entertaining such improper notions when it was the girl's sister he was supposed to be courting?

Chapter 9

"You look right pretty, miss."

Hannah surveyed herself in the cheval glass while Lily gave one more fluff to the puffed sleeves of Hannah's ball gown. Truth be told, she did look rather fine. She had fussed and complained when Charlotte had ordered the dress and forced her to stand still for fitting after fitting. She was glad now her sister had gone to such trouble. She really felt very grown-up.

"I must go see to her ladyship now," Lily said.

Charlotte had agreed that Hannah might share Lily while at Epping Hall. Fortunately for the overworked girl, Hannah never required much from a maid. But tonight, for her first real ball, she was loathe to let the maid go.

"Are you sure I do not look like a Bartholomew doll?"

Lily chuckled. "No, miss. You look very pretty."

"Are you certain I am not showing too much bosom?" She tugged at the blond lace trim along the low-cut neckline. "I have never worn anything quite this daring. I can't imagine Charlotte thinks this to be proper for me. I am not a dashing widow, after all."

"It is the fashion, miss," Lily said, readjusting the lace. "And it looks very well on you."

"But what about this thing?" Hannah asked, reaching up to finger the fillet that held her hair in place. It was made of twisted bands of stiffened satin and seed pearls, and sat tightly on her head like an open cap, her masses of dark curls spilling all around it. "Are you sure this will work?"

"It is perfect, miss," Lily said, gently coaxing Hannah's hand down. "And it is secure enough to hold the curls in place."

"Even mine? Nothing ever seems to hold my hair in place." Hannah reached up again to nervously finger the headpiece. If pins couldn't hold her hair, how was this little bit of fabric supposed to do it? "Perhaps we should have used combs instead. Or perhaps I ought to have had it cropped."

"Oh no, miss. That would be a right shame. Other ladies would sell their souls for your natural curls." Lily once again coaxed Hannah's hands away from her coiffure. "Now, if you'll just stand nice and straight," Lily continued, "hold your head up tall—that's it— then everything should stay in place, all right and tight. So long as you don't get too lively during the country dances!"

Even the maid knew more about proper behavior than she did.

"Now, I really must go to her ladyship."

"Of course, Lily, go on to Charlotte. And thank you ever so much. I declare I feel fine as five pence. I shall not move a muscle until it's time to go down."

If only she could get through the rest of the evening without moving a muscle. One of the tricks to being a lady, she suspected, was to move as little as necessary so as to maintain the condition of one's dress and coiffure. Or, at the very least, to sit and stand and move and dance only in such a way as to cause as little damage as possible.

To preserve the lovely coiffure Lily had created, Hannah would make an effort to be conscious of her fillet at all times—not such a difficult task since the wretched thing pinched.

The dress was another matter. The straighter she stood—to keep the fillet in place—the more pronounced her overexposed bosom became. It was probably not a ladylike thing to be tugging at one's lace all evening. Perhaps she could borrow a fan and keep it spread appropriately. Of course, that would not be possible if she was asked to dance.

Which brought to mind another problem with the dress. It hung low in the back so that when she walked it gave the impression of a train. Not a real train that could be attached to her wrist and kept out of the way during the dancing. Just a hint of a train that skimmed the floor. Charlotte and the modiste claimed it was all the crack. She sent up a silent prayer that her unruly feet would not get tangled up in all that satin.

Hannah stood and stared at her reflection in the cheval glass. I look like a real lady, she thought, bosom and all. Now, if she could only act like a lady, the evening would be a success. Charlotte would be proud of her.

And maybe, just maybe, the earl would notice. Despite his kind words at Oundle—he was merely being polite to a houseguest—she felt ashamed of the bad opinion he must have of her. Tonight she wanted him to think her a real lady. For Charlotte's sake.

Determined to live up to her ladylike appearance, Hannah mentally repeated the litany drummed into her head so often by Charlotte.

Think before you speak.

Keep responses brief and do not ramble.

Do not use stable cant or other inappropriate language.

Do not mention books or architecture or St. Biddulph's.

Stick to safe subjects, like the weather.

Stand up straight.

Do not laugh out loud.

Do not bounce or march heavily when walking, but glide gracefully.

Do not refuse any gentleman's offer to dance.

Do not agree to dance a waltz.

Do not dance with any gentleman more than twice.

Do not step on a gentleman's toes.

Do not . . . Do not . . . Do not . . .

It was too much. "I cannot do it!" Hannah wailed aloud to her reflection.

"Cannot do what?"

Hannah gave a start as Cousin Winifred swept into the room. "I'm sorry, my dear. I did knock, but apparently you did not hear. My goodness, don't you look lovely. Now, tell me what it is you cannot do."

Winifred circled Hannah, closely examining every detail of her dress, nodding her approval.

"Cousin Winifred," Hannah said, standing still under the older woman's inspection, "I want so much to please Charlotte tonight. I want to be a real lady."

"You look like a real lady to me, my dear. Did Charlotte choose the dress for you?"

"Yes, ma'am."

"She did very well, then. It is quite charming. The sleeves are marvelous." Winifred carefully fingered the slashed blue satin sleeves with a darker blue peeking through, finished on the edges with a simple fall of blond lace. "And the fillet sets them off beautifully." The twisted satin band was composed of both shades of blue. "The whole ensemble quite becomes you, my dear. Now, what makes you think you cannot be a real lady?"

Winifred, clad in a stunning bronze gown, perched gingerly on the edge of a delicate painted chair. Hannah watched her movements. Here was a real lady, sitting carefully to preserve her gown. When Winifred had finished arranging her skirts, she looked up at Hannah and lifted her brows in question.

"I am trying to remember all the rules of being a lady," Hannah said, her voice sounding overwrought even to her own ears. "But there are too many of them! How can I possibly stand tall and say all the right things and keep my curls in place and try not to trip over my feet all at the same time?"

"Hannah, my dear girl, you must stop trying so hard." Winifred's eyes softened with such compassion Hannah could easily have thrown herself onto the woman's breast and sobbed. But that would ruin both their gowns, so she kept her place before the mirror.

"You have always been a young lady," Winifred continued. "You were born and bred to it. You have a lady's education, and more. You have a lady's manners—I have yet to see you wipe your face on the tablecloth or spit into a corner. I've seen you pour tea and sketch and read to the children. You're compassionate, intelligent, and—"

"Unpolished."

Winifred waved her hand in a dismissive gesture. "Perhaps a little," she said. "But you have all the makings of a true lady. Besides, several of the grandest ladies I know have some very rough edges indeed. Don't try to polish away everything that makes you special."

Hannah shrugged. "The earl said almost the same thing."

Winifred's brows rose, as though astonished. "Did he, indeed?" She tapped her lips with a gloved finger and scrutinized Hannah from head to toe. "Well, what do you know about that?" she muttered.

"I beg your pardon?"

Winifred chuckled. "It is just that my brother and I seldom see eye to eye. On this, we are agreed. You are a delightful young lady, my dear, and must not try so hard to be something else."

"Lottie says I am willful and headstrong."

"Oh, I think young and high-spirited better describes you. Plain-spoken, yes. Unaffected, too—but there is a certain charm in that. Untried and therefore a tad unsophisticated. But all that will fade with time and experience. Just be yourself, my dear, and don't concentrate so hard on all those so-called rules."

"There are too many of them to keep straight in any case," Hannah said. "I have more or less decided to focus my attention on keeping my fillet and coiffure in place. If the confounded thing slips and my curls go tumbling down, who will even notice my fine new dress or my demure conversation?"

"An admirable goal," Winifred said with a smile as Hannah practiced her stance before the cheval glass. "With your lovely neck stretched up and back upon your straight shoulders, my dear Hannah, you look as regal as any queen."

Hannah burst into laughter and spoiled the effect. "Oh, Cousin Winifred," she said, recalling one of her other dilemmas, "do you think I ought to use a fan? To cover up . . ." She waved a hand in front of her bosom.

"Good heavens, why?"

"You are sure it is not a bit . . . a bit too revealing?"

"My dear girl, I assure you every woman at the ball will be equally revealed. It is the fashion." She looked down at her own less than ample bosom and laughed. "I promise you, if I weren't as skinny as a nail, this dress would be a lot more provocative. You are blessed, my girl. Be grateful. Be proud. Stand tall. And enjoy yourself."

Hannah gave a bark of laughter, then quickly covered her mouth. She must remember: Ladies do not laugh out loud.

What a tiresome bunch ladies were, to be sure.

"Thank you, Cousin Winifred. You have quite cheered me up. I believe I am ready to face the evening. Fillet in place. Shall we go?"

* * *

Where was Hannah? Miles scanned the ballroom—
actually the Long Gallery cleared of excess furniture
and rugs, and redefined as a ballroom—in search of
her. He wanted to reserve a set. She looked remarkably
pretty this evening. Remarkably pretty.

Joseph, bless the man, had led Hannah out for the
opening set. George had led out a glowing Rachel
Wetherby. Things were looking well in that quarter.
Though Miles had danced with Charlotte—magnificent in a deep green silk gown that clung to every
curve—his gaze had frequently strayed in the direction of Hannah. She looked very . . . what? Mature?
No, not quite that. Eyes sparkling with undisguised
enjoyment, dimples winking up at Joseph, she still
looked very much the young girl.

And yet, not so young. The low-cut dress showed
her to be every inch a woman. Amazing what the right
gown and a sophisticated hair style could do.

Hannah looked beautiful, and he felt proud for her.
In a brotherly sort of way, of course.

Each time he had met Charlotte in the progressive
country dance that opened the ball, she had captured
his attention thoroughly. Her enticing gown with its
incredibly abbreviated bodice, revealed a great deal of
her charms. The gown was designed to attract men
like a magnet, and Miles was not immune to that attraction.

But when the pattern called for her to be handed off
to another gentleman, or while standing in line watching another couple progress down the set, Miles found
himself looking down the line toward Joseph and
Hannah. She danced well. There was an air of gaiety
about her that he envied. Her boundless energy was
almost foreign to him. Had he ever been that young
and gay?

Miles had missed the second set in order to greet a group of late arrivals, but he had glanced frequently in Hannah's direction as she stepped through a lively reel with George. Joseph, true to form, had secured Charlotte for the second set. Charlotte frequently drew Miles's eyes as well. How could she not? She was easily the most beautiful woman at the ball.

But more often, it was Hannah he watched. He was pleased to see her enjoying herself. She had been so quiet and reserved during the last week—with the exception of the brief hour she had spent with him at St. Peter's in Oundle—he had worried that Charlotte's scoldings had begun to wear Hannah down. Poor thing, she had been so concerned about behaving like a lady. Yet this evening, she was a lady in every way. And remarkably pretty.

Charlotte must be proud. If he married her, he would offer his home to Hannah as well. Until she married. He would miss her liveliness and her cock-eyed charm, otherwise.

Miles had been engaged for the next set with Lady Beddowes, whose husband's estate in the southern part of the county was said by some to rival Epping Hall. Not by the Earl of Strickland, to be sure, but by a few other less discerning observers. The viscountess had kept up a steady stream of conversation that did not allow Miles's attention to stray for a moment. He did, though, catch sight of Hannah as she progressed down the line next to his, on the arm of young Rufus Mayfield, one of the many sons of Lord Oliver Mayfield of Leicestershire.

Miles hoped to engage her for this set, or at least reserve a later set.

But where was she? She wasn't dancing, of that he was sure. Had some cad swept her out onto the terrace already?

Lord, but he was beginning to sound more and more like her stern older brother.

He could not imagine her wandering off for some romantic interlude. More likely, knowing Hannah, she had torn her dress and had gone to repair it.

Miles made his way along the edges of the gallery, stopping to say a word now and then to one of the guests. Finally, he spotted her. She stood half concealed by one of the marble pillars that separated the Long Gallery from the series of anterooms in the adjacent wing.

He smiled to note that she swayed slightly with the music, one foot softly beating time. She held a fan and worked it vigorously. There was nothing coy in her use of it. Hannah probably had no idea how to use a fan in that way. There was no guile in her faint smile and brisk fanning. She was simply cooling herself after several strenuous country dances.

He walked toward her. She saw his approach and flashed him a dazzling smile that seemed to catch him hard beneath the ribs.

Then Hannah stepped away from the pillar.

At that moment, a footman carrying a large tray of wineglasses turned into the gallery from the first anteroom. He obviously had not seen Hannah until she stepped away from the pillar. And neither did Hannah see the footman.

The two collided with the force of surprise. The footman bobbled his tray. Hannah recoiled, stepping backward. Her foot appeared to become snagged in her demi-train. Reaching blindly, her neck and shoulders oddly stiff, she grabbed at the footman. Both went tumbling to the floor in a mess of broken glass and spilled wine.

It had all happened in an instant. Miles had not stopped moving forward, but by the time he reached them, the footman and Hannah were both sprawled and dazed amid the debris.

He rushed to her side.

"Hannah! Are you hurt?" She had landed rather awkwardly—and no doubt painfully—on her bottom. She shook her head, but neither spoke nor looked up. Poor girl. He didn't know whether to laugh—it was so typically Hannah he could have predicted the entire incident—or cry for her obvious mortification.

"Hannah?" Miles reached out a hand to help her up. She sat quite still for a moment, then lifted a hand to touch her hair. Finally, she looked up, but not at Miles, then took his hand. He tugged her awkwardly to her feet, steadied her, then turned to deal with the footman.

The boy was unhurt but scarlet with embarrassment, muttering apology after apology, and asking if the young lady was all right.

Miles looked to Hannah to find her beautiful blue satin gown stained burgundy all down one side. Her eyes brimmed. Her lip trembled.

"I will see to the lady," Miles said to the footman. "Get some help to clean up this mess before another accident occurs."

"Yes, my lord."

Miles looked about to see how large an audience they had attracted. His first thought was of Charlotte, but she, thank God, was nowhere in sight. Fortunately, few guests had witnessed the incident, this being one of the least frequented areas of the room during the early part of the evening. In a few hours, when supper was served in the anterooms, the place would be swarming with guests.

Miles took Hannah by the elbow and steered her away from the gallery. She choked back a sob.

"I'm such a c-clod," she said. "I c-can't do anything right."

Chapter 10

Hannah wanted to die.

She prayed for the floor to split open with a huge fissure that would swallow her up, then close tight behind her.

"Hush, now," the earl said in a gentle voice. She had begun to whimper like a child. He led her firmly by the arm through a series of anterooms where servants scurried about setting up buffet tables for the late supper.

The worst part of the whole nightmare, the very worst part, was that it had happened in front of him. The elegant, dignified Lord Strickland. The very last person she would have wanted to witness such a bone-headed, clumsy, appalling catastrophe.

With the possible exception of Charlotte.

If he had already thought her graceless and gauche, what must he think of her now?

And therein lay the source of her despair: She cared what he thought. When had she ever cared what people thought of her? Before she had begun this foolish attempt to be a lady, such a moronic mishap would not have discomposed her even for a moment. But it did now. Because of him.

She could not look at him. She could never look him in the eye again without wanting to die.

It had been such a magical evening. From the moment Hannah had entered the gallery—when everyone had smiled and lavished her with compliments—she had felt like a lady. A real lady.

Even Major Prescott's flirting seemed a little less disingenuous than usual. He had studied her impertinently from head to toe and pronounced her beautiful. She almost believed him.

Charlotte had surprised her several times with an affectionate smile, which could only mean that for once she, too, was pleased with Hannah.

She hadn't made any mistakes. Remembering to concentrate on her fillet, the rest had come surprisingly easy. She had moved through three dances, had performed the steps perfectly, and hadn't stumbled once. As far as she could tell, she had not blurted out anything improper or embarrassed anyone with an ill-mannered remark. What with the dancing and all, there had been little time for conversation.

And, oh, how she loved to dance! The last time she could recall dancing was at a small local assembly some months before her mother's death. She had almost forgotten what fun it was to get caught up in the music and the patterns of movement.

All in all, it was a glorious evening. She had moved to the far end of the gallery only to lean against the cool marble of a pillar and try to catch her breath. While she fanned herself, Hannah wondered if the earl had seen her and been as pleased as Charlotte appeared to be.

And suddenly, there he was, walking toward her and smiling. How she had hoped he was going to ask her to dance! It had been difficult to keep her eyes off him all evening. He looked magnificent in black evening clothes. So handsome. So refined. Even while dancing with others, she had stolen glance after glance in the earl's direction.

It wasn't right that she should take such an interest in her sister's future husband. She knew it was wrong, but she could not help it. He was just about the most wonderful man she'd ever met.

She had to go careening into a footman and fall on her bum in front of this perfect man.

What a silly cow she was for believing the magic of the evening could last.

She wanted to die.

"This way, Hannah." The earl led her beyond the supper rooms and into a small salon of some sort. A fire burned in the grate, in preparation for wandering guests. Thankfully, the room was presently empty.

The earl released her arm and Hannah went to stand by the fire. He swung the door closed, then apparently remembered who she was and left it slightly ajar. Ever the proper gentleman.

He stood across the room with his hands behind his back. Flickering light from a nearby wall sconce cast shadows in the chiseled hollows of his cheeks and the angles of his jaw. "Are you certain you are all right?" he asked.

No, she was not all right. "I just want to die," she heard herself say.

"Ah, Hannah. Please do not be so distressed. It was an unfortunate accident witnessed by almost no one."

Except you.

"I do not like to hear you say that you cannot do anything right," he continued. "You know that is not true."

"But look at me!" She held her hands out to her sides, palms up. "Look what a mess I've made of everything."

He took a step closer into the room. "It is indeed a pity about the dress," he said. "You looked lovely tonight."

Oh, God. He was too kind. She wanted to cry.

"I was trying so hard," she said, her voice sinking to a whisper of anguished shame.

He took another step toward her, watching her with the aristocratic reserve that had become so familiar. His height often caused him to appear to be looking down his nose at one, emphasizing the impression of detached aloofness. The only real communication came from his eyes. Others, including Charlotte, could not see beyond the lordly aspect. If only they would watch his eyes, she had often thought, they would see the true man. They would see beyond the formal manners to his gentleness and compassion. They would see beyond the stiff dignity to his wry sense of humor. They would see how wonderful he was.

Did Charlotte realize how wonderful he was?

At the moment, she saw such kindness in those brown eyes that she wanted to drown in them. She could not tear her gaze away. His eyes seemed to welcome her in, and unguarded words of misery and humiliation poured out of her in the most unladylike fashion.

"I tried so hard," she said, unable to control the quaver in her voice. "I wanted to be a real lady for once. For tonight, I did not want to be dismissed as a schoolgirl. I wanted to be grown-up. I wanted to be a lady." She took a shuddery breath. "I confess, I felt quite splendid in my new dress. I really did. Everything was going so well, and I was having such a good time. But it couldn't last. There were too many rules!" Her voice had risen in pitch and she was on the verge of wailing. "I told Cousin Winifred I would never be able to concentrate on them all. But I wanted to make Charlotte proud and—"

"I am certain your sister was proud," he said, mercifully interrupting before she could admit how much she had wanted to please him as well. "You looked very pretty and danced beautifully. Why, even Winifred pulled me aside to be sure I had noticed how lovely you looked."

Oh, Lord, she was going to cry. Not now. Not now. Please, not now. Not in front of him.

"Hannah, I watched you all evening—"

He had?

"—and you behaved like a perfect lady. I didn't see you trip over your feet during any of the dances. It was not your fault that a clumsy footman plowed into you."

"But he might have remained upright if I hadn't been concentrating so hard on the blasted fillet so that I didn't notice I'd stepped on my skirt, and I wouldn't have lost my balance and pulled him down with me!"

"What blasted fillet?"

"This wretched thing!" She pointed to her head-piece. "I'll wager it's still in place, too."

"The twisted band in your hair? Yes, it seems to be in place. I noticed earlier how pretty it looked."

"And so I've ruined my beautiful dress but maintained my coiffure. What does that make me, half a lady? A lady from the neck up? No, that can't be true because that would include my mouth, and no one can say there is anything ladylike about my unruly tongue that I cannot seem to check even at this moment." Humiliation burned hot on her cheeks. "So the only part of me that succeeded as a lady is the top of my head. The rest of me . . . the rest of me is a failure."

With that, she burst into tears.

Mortified, she dropped her face into her hands and sobbed. She had never been more miserable in all her life. And *he* had to witness it. As long as she kept her eyes covered, she could pretend he wasn't there. Perhaps he would go away and leave her alone with her shame.

But the next thing she knew, strong arms were enfolding her, and she found her head buried against a warm, broad shoulder.

*   *   *

He held her gently and let her cry. She sounded so miserable, poor girl. And yet somehow he felt like laughing. It was strange how often she made him want to laugh. Here she was, all dressed up and coiffed in her ladylike best, and yet she was still Hannah, tripping over her feet and giving heedless voice to her every thought with no concern that she probably ought not to speak so openly to a man she'd known only a few weeks. Most girls her age would never have dreamed of admitting aloud to the insecurities and self-doubts she had just acknowledged.

He found himself muttering sounds of comfort, soothing little nonsense words that he used when Amy was upset.

But Hannah was no little girl.

And he was not at all sure it was a good idea to be holding her as though she were. Miles's emotions were a jumble of protectiveness, amusement, and reluctant desire. The latter was not at all in keeping with the consoling, wise older brother figure he had meant to present.

Yet, her soft body leaning into his own made it difficult to ignore those traitorous feelings. Her hands were fortunately pressed flat against his chest, shielding the full breasts he had noticed tonight for the first time. He did not like to think how he might react to closer contact with them.

Miles closed his eyes and thought of Amy and of Charlotte and of honor and integrity.

"Oh, m-my lord, I am s-so ash-sh-shamed," she sputtered against his shoulder.

"Shh," he said, gently rubbing one hand up and down her upper back, the way he did when Amy cried.

"B-but I never c-cry. It is s-so emb-b-barrassing."

"Do not be embarrassed, Hannah. It is only me."

She uttered a choking kind of snort.

"You needed a shoulder to cry on, and I am happy to oblige," he said, wondering for a moment about the state of his neckcloth.

"You are v-very k-kind, my lord." She took one long shuddery breath and the tears seemed to subside a bit. The storm had passed. He continued to hold her while she collected herself.

After a long silence, she said, "Oh, how I wish my m-mother were here."

"You miss her."

"Of course."

"And what do you suppose she would say to you if she were here right now?"

Hannah hiccuped and raised her head from his shoulder. It was almost disconcerting the way she always looked one squarely in the eye like that, usually followed by some blunt statement of opinion. She leaned away from him and cocked her head to one side.

"She would laugh."

"Your mother would have laughed at you?"

"Not at me, exactly, but at what happens to me. Or at the things I do. I was a constant source of amusement to her."

Good Lord, had her mother made fun of her? Her own mother? His disbelief must have registered on his face.

"No, no, my lord, it was not what you are thinking. Mother was not cruel. She loved me. And I adored her. Since I was first able to talk, I have been chattering a blue streak and blurting out every idea and opinion that popped into my head. Although Charlotte has scolded me often enough for not knowing when to keep silent, Mother never tried to curb my tongue. More often than not, she would burst out laughing."

She sniffed and gave a wistful little smile.

"And she did not care that the sorts of things that interested other girls did not interest me. Or that I was clumsy. She told me I marched to a different drummer, and that was fine with her so long as I was happy. She said I was an original. She always made me feel very special."

She closed her eyes for a moment, and when she opened them, they glistened with tears again. "She would have laughed. She would have laughed and told me to change my dress and go back to the ball and have a good time."

Miles looked down into those moist blue eyes that could drive a sane man to distraction. Seemingly of its own volition, his hand reached up and brushed away a tear from her flushed cheek, then ran a finger under her chin and tilted it up.

"Your mother was very wise," he said in a suddenly husky voice. "And absolutely right. You are indeed very special, Hannah Fairbanks."

He bent his head and tugged her chin closer. He could smell the faint fragrance of soap. Nothing exotic. Just clean, humble soap. All at once it was the most intoxicating scent he'd ever known. It drew him closer. Closer. Her breath whispered across his face like a caress. His gaze dropped to her lips, full and pink and slightly parted. He moved closer. Closer.

"My lord?"

Her whispered words caused him to blink. Her look of wide-eyed confusion brought him to his senses.

My God. What was he doing?

Miles dropped his hand from her chin. His other hand still rested lightly on her waist. He pulled it away as though scalded, then stepped back toward the middle of the room.

What the devil had got into him? He had almost kissed her, for God's sake. A young innocent girl, a guest in his home, the sister of the woman he courted. Had he lost all sense of propriety?

He had meant only to comfort her in her distress. He had never intended anything more.

Except for one irrational moment, when she had become so utterly and completely adorable he had been ready to abandon all that was proper and kiss her.

Hannah stood across the room looking so bewildered, Miles thanked heaven he had not given into temptation. She was too young. She had no experience with men. She could not understand how provocative youth and innocence can sometimes be. Especially to a man who had been too long without a woman, so that when he found one in his arms, she became almost irresistible.

She probably had no idea what had almost just happened. He hoped.

"Yes, your mother was right," he said, brushing a piece of lint off his sleeve and retreating to a more formal tone of voice. "You must not let this foolish incident spoil your evening." *Foolish, indeed.* "You must change your dress and return to the ball. It is early yet."

Hannah looked down at her ruined gown and made a face. "I don't know. I think I'd prefer to return to my room and study my notes on St. Biddulph's."

"Ah, but you must return. I shall be disappointed if you do not. And I am sure your sister would be very displeased."

She heaved a sigh and shook our her stained skirt. "I am sure you are right. Blast it all!"

"I shall have one of the footmen alert your maid. Her name is . . . ?"

"Lily."

"I shall have a message sent to Lily to come to your bedchamber at once to help you."

"Thank you, my lord. You have been . . . most kind."

"Yes, well." Miles cleared his throat nervously. "Do you know the way?"

"Yes."

"I shall leave you then, in hopes of seeing you back at the ball shortly."

He gave her a stiff bow and left the room. He gave brief instructions to a passing footman regarding Hannah's maid, then continued on his way. When he reached the pillars at the end of the Long Gallery, he paused and took a deep breath. He had almost made a grievous mistake this evening. Kissing Hannah would not have been like kissing her sister. Because of her youth and inexperience, he would have felt obligated to offer for Hannah.

Adorable as she might be, she was not at all the sort of wife he wanted. Not at all.

Miles checked his neckcloth in a nearby pier glass. The arrangement was no longer pristine, but it would do. He straightened his shoulders and walked into the Long Gallery. He would find Lady Abingdon and maneuver her into a dark corner and kiss her properly. She would help him forget what had almost happened with Hannah.

Chapter 11

Hannah watched the earl leave, then fell back into a chair near the fire. Literally fell. Her knees would no longer support her. She could not even manage to lift a hand to wipe the tears that spilled down her cheeks.

She had thought he was going to kiss her.

For a brief moment, when the world stood still and the music from the ball was drowned out by the pounding of her heart, she had imagined the unthinkable. She had let herself believe the Earl of Strickland, her sister's beau, would kiss her.

She had wanted him to kiss her. It frightened and embarrassed her how much she wanted it, would have welcomed it. And she would have kissed him back.

It was an absurd notion, of course. Kissing her had probably been the furthest thing from his mind. Why on earth would he have wanted to kiss someone like her? And how horribly disloyal to Charlotte to have even considered it.

Worse still—much, much worse—was that when he had told her she was special and gazed into her eyes with a look that had thrown her heart into a wild disorder, she had done something very foolish, something unforgivable. She had fallen irrevocably in love with him.

Stupid, stupid girl!

Everyone thought her childish. Well, she felt terribly childish at the moment, pining after a man she could

never have and had no right to be worshiping even
from afar. He was not available. He was going to
marry Charlotte, her own sister.

Dear God, was she doomed to spend the rest of her
life secretly in love with her brother-in-law?

Hannah groaned aloud and dropped her head into
her hands. What kind of an idiot had she become? It
was not as if the earl cared for her in any way other
than that of a sort of older brother. She had simply
misinterpreted kindness for something else.

When she had been wrapped in his arms, she
thought she would never want to be any other place
ever again. It had felt like heaven. He had felt like
heaven—strong and tall and well muscled. She had
never before been so conscious of a man's physical
presence. His heart had beat steadily beneath her
hands as they lay flat against his chest. His chin had
nudged the side of her head. His hands had worked
magic along her back.

A pang of something she had never felt before and
could not identify coiled low in her belly.

He was only being kind to a foolish young girl who
behaved like a ninny. He would have done the same
for anyone. He had told her she was special, but he
had simply been trying to make her feel better. He had
not gazed longingly into her eyes. He had studied her
face to see if she had recovered. He had not been about
to kiss her.

Stupid, stupid girl! Had he known what she expected? Had she made a complete fool of herself?

Of all the men in the world to finally pique her interest, why did it have to be this man? Why now?

Hannah had never in all her life been interested in
love or courtship or romance. It had all seemed so
much nonsense, and of no great importance in the
overall scheme of things. There had always been so
many more important matters to consider, like the late

Saxon development of nave aisles in relation to the earlier use of porticus. Or how Carolingian influences had altered the Romano-British basilica with the introduction of transepts and rounded apses.

Her studies had simply proven infinitely more interesting than romantic fantasies about gentlemen. But perhaps she simply had not met the right gentleman.

Until now.

Of course, he was not the right gentleman at all. He was as wrong a gentleman as he could be. He had certainly caused her to engage in uncharacteristic fantasies. How could she have even pretended such a man would ever want to kiss her? He was noble and dignified and as blue-blooded as they came, and she was cloddish, clumsy, and naïve. What a splendid pair they would make.

Even so, she had fallen in love with him as surely as she'd fallen out of the tree that day by the lake.

There was nothing for it now but to put as much distance between herself and the earl as possible. She would not wait for a wedding. She would write to her half brother, Bertram, and beg him to take her in. It was not as though she were destitute. She would not be throwing herself upon his mercy as a poor relation. Hannah had inherited her mother's modest fortune. She simply needed Bertram and his wife to lend her propriety until she was old enough to set up her own establishment.

The problem was, Bertram did not like her very much. He was more of a high stickler than even Charlotte. He would likely make her life a misery. But it would be preferable to the heartache of facing the earl every day as Charlotte's husband.

She would think about writing Bertram tomorrow. Or perhaps the next day. She still had much to do at St. Biddulph's before she could consider leaving Epping

Hall. It should be easy enough to avoid the earl and Charlotte by spending all her time at the church.

Hannah pushed herself off the chair and walked to the door of the salon. She peered out into the ante-room, but saw only servants milling about. Bunching her skirt as much as possible to hide the huge stain down one side, she left the room.

When she reached her bedchamber, Lily stood just inside waiting for her.

"Oh, miss!" she exclaimed. "Your beautiful dress! What happened?"

"I collided with a tray of wineglasses," Hannah replied. "It had to be claret, of course, and not cham-pagne, which would have done less damage. Is it ru-ined beyond hope, do you think?"

Lily held out the skirt and examined the stain closely. "Perhaps not, miss," she said. "Sometimes warm milk takes out a wine stain. Here, let me help you out of it, then I'll take it down to the laundry and see what I can do."

"Oh, do not trouble yourself tonight, Lily. Just see if you can find me another dress that looks halfway de-cent."

Lily went to the clothespress and opened one of its flanking hanging cupboards. She riffled through the dresses that hung on pegs, rejecting one after the other with a shake of her head. It was not until she had begun to sort through the second cupboard that she found something suitable.

"Here is the rose figured silk, miss," she said. "It should do very well."

Hannah had already worn that dress one evening, but she had no other ball dress, so the rose silk would have to do.

"But then I'll need to restyle your hair," Lily said. "The blue fillet would not look right with the rose silk."

"Blasted fillet," Hannah muttered.

Lily helped her out of her ruined dress only to discover her undergarments were also stained. It was necessary to redress from the skin out. Once the new dress was in place, Lily brought forth a cluster of pink silk flowers that she pinned to the bodice.

"This silk posy will help to fancy it up a bit," Lily said. "And I'm sure her ladyship won't mind lending it to you for the evening."

The talented maid then set about dismantling Hannah's perfect coiffure. This time she wove pink ribbons through the curls, cunningly tying them in an elaborate knot at the back to anchor the arrangement of curls in place.

Lily assured her that she looked as fine as before, but Hannah did not believe a word of it. Neither did she care. The evening was already ruined, and her heart was already broken. What difference did a dress make?

"Thank you, Lily. Now, let's see how long this one lasts."

She made her way back to the Long Gallery, entering through the supper rooms, hoping to be unnoticed. She had taken no more than two steps when she spied Charlotte dancing with Lord Beddowes. As luck would have it, Hannah caught Charlotte's eye.

Without missing a step or dropping her smile, Charlotte sent a clear message of reproach. Even across the width of the room, her every muscle and sinew strained to project disapproval.

If she was upset about a change of dress, how would she react if she knew her sister had fallen in love with Lord Strickland?

Hannah would never have to face the answer to that question, for she would never reveal her secret. Not to a living soul. She would rather die first.

*   *   *

"So you see, I've made rather a mess of things, my love." Miles paced back and forth in the Lady Chapel of St. Biddulph's. The pale light of a gray morning did little to illuminate the small chapel. He needed no light. He knew every inch of the place. He had tried to sit, but fidgeted and couldn't stay still.

"I know that Lady Abingdon would make a fine wife, but I just cannot do it. I thought I could, but I cannot. Not now. Not after last night."

As planned, he had sought out Charlotte late in the ball and got her alone, hoping to slake those inappropriate stirrings he had felt with Hannah. But he couldn't do it.

He had the woman in his arms, and she was more than ready to cooperate. Instead, he had looked into her bedroom eyes and felt absolutely nothing. No, that was not correct. He had felt something. He had felt it was wrong, all wrong. She was not the one he wanted in his arms.

He had pulled away, muttered an apology for his impertinence, and left the lady standing alone in the darkened alcove.

"It seems odd to be telling you of my failed attempt at an amorous encounter, Amelia. But I felt such a cad. In that moment I knew without hesitation that Charlotte was not the woman I wanted. To kiss her again would only move me closer to being obliged to make her an offer. Under the circumstances, it would be difficult to live with that mistake."

He circled the perimeter of the small chapel, reaching out to touch a carved angel on his mother's tomb, to run a finger along Sir John's sword, to trace a line in the dust along some unknown ancestor's grave marker.

"It is not that I want to marry Hannah," he continued. "I do not. She is not the right woman for me, either. She is much too young and too unconventional. It is just not right that I should harbor secret feelings of desire for the younger sister of my wife. How could I live with that? I confess, it shook me to my boots when I became aware of the attraction. It was so unexpected."

He stopped in front of a bench, sat down, then got up again, walked to the window, and walked back to stand before Amelia's tomb. He opened his mouth to speak, but did not. He turned and began pacing the chapel in the opposite direction.

"God, I am so ashamed." The sound of his voice bounced off the old stone walls. He lowered his tone to a whisper. "I was worried about Win and everyone else pushing me into a commitment with Charlotte, I had not even noticed it was Hannah who had captured my interest. But dammit, she is little more than a child."

An image came into his mind of the full, round bosom revealed by her ball gown. The soft shoulders. The long elegant neck set off by the upswept hairstyle.

"If not precisely a child, then certainly a green girl. No, despite my unspeakable behavior, Hannah is not the one for me." He slowed to run his fingers along the carved letters of Amelia's name, then resumed his pace.

"Oh, but she is delightful, my love. I wish you could know her. I have never laughed as much as I have since she arrived. She is full of life. And it is not mere youthfulness. It comes from the core of her, somehow. It defines her. I suspect she will have as much vitality in forty or fifty years, and still be poking around in her old churches with boundless enthusiasm."

It was that vitality, he realized, that most attracted him.

"I've told you before that I envy Hannah, the way

she says whatever she wants to whomever she wants and cares little for the opinion of others."

Except for last night when she seemed concerned with what he thought of her.

"Ah, to be that free. You are the only one, my dear, with whom I have ever felt at liberty to be that completely open. Oh, there are George and Nigel and Winifred, of course. And good friends like Joseph and Stephen. But I was never as completely free and open with any of them as I was with you."

Miles was very much aware that he wore his position and rank like a uniform, feeling obliged to be His Lordship and to behave accordingly. Such behavior had been bred into him from birth, as heir to his father's title and fortune. He had never, even as a young child, learned to be spontaneous or frivolous, unlike the rest of his siblings. Every step taken and every word spoken was done with the consciousness of rank and dignity.

Perhaps that was one of the reasons he had so fallen apart at Amelia's death. She had been the one person in the world with whom he could strip all layers of nobility and position and be totally free, unfettered by the need to be The Earl and able to be just Miles, the man.

Was that why Charlotte was so wrong for him, because he could never imagine himself so uninhibited with her?

He should not begin to hope for such liberty with a second wife. It was not to be expected. It came with loving, and that was not possible again.

Hannah came close to stripping him of his dignity. But that was not the same thing at all.

He stood at the window again, leaning against the embrasure and rocking back and forth on his heels.

"Hannah is, of course, wonderful with the girls," he continued, "and will make a good mother one day.

Amy practically worships her. Follows her every-where. Hannah has brought our little Amy out of her shell at last. It is quite remarkable, my love. I wish you could see her. Oh, she is still petulant and pouty at times, but less so since Hannah arrived. And she has learned to laugh again."

Whatever else happened, Miles would always be grateful for the changes Hannah had wrought with Amy.

"But just because I've decided against Charlotte does not mean I've decided in favor of Hannah. We would never suit. She is patently headstrong and out-spoken. If she is unconventional in youth, she will likely to be a certified eccentric as she gets older."

Miles pushed away from the window and stepped over to a molded wall recess that held the tomb of his great-great grandfather, the seventh earl. Old Edward had been the last true eccentric in the Prescott line. Succeeding generations had become pattern cards of propriety, culminating in himself—the starchiest, dullest, most punctilious of the lot.

No eccentric countess for this earl.

"No, she is much too young," he said. "Recollect, if you will, my intentions of taking an older woman for a second wife. That resolution stands firm. Young girls are looking for something I cannot give. Despite her protestations against marriage, Hannah no doubt has the same dreams of love and romance as other girls her age. It would be extraordinary if she did not. But she would find none of those things with me. As you know, I am no longer capable of giving them."

There was no need to repeat this justification of his intentions. He had been over and over it a thousand times. And with all due respect to Amelia, he had to leave. He was so restless and edgy, he did not know what was wrong with him.

But this tiny chapel could not contain him at the moment. He needed to ride. He would have his horse saddled and go for a long gallop. That should relieve him of the fidgets.

"I must be off, Amelia. I apologize for being in such a sorry state today. Perhaps tomorrow I will be more myself. Good-bye for now, my dear."

It was not until later when he'd ridden hell for leather halfway across his lands that he realized he'd forgotten to tell Amelia that he loved her.

Chapter 12

The many wonders of St. Biddulph's proved to be a welcome antidote to the malaise that drained Hannah in the days following the Epping ball.

Nighttime was the worst time, when she lay sleepless in her bed, plagued with thoughts of the earl and how it had felt to be held in his arms. Or tormented with guilt over her disloyalty to Charlotte. It did not matter that Hannah had never believed her sister and the earl to be suitably matched. It was none of her concern and certainly gave her no right to try and make a match for herself.

But that was not what she sought at all. She never had and never would believe that the earl could ever think of her in such a way. She knew what he thought of her. She had given him every opportunity to see her as a clumsy, uncouth child.

It was not his fault that she had fallen in love with him. He had not encouraged it. She had not meant for it to happen. It was just something she was going to have to ignore. Like any childish infatuation, she would get over it.

Evenings were difficult when she could not avoid the company of Charlotte or Lord Strickland. She spoke as little as possible during meals, and excused herself from the drawing room after supper in order to read or sketch.

No one seemed to miss her.

Charlotte was too preoccupied with the progress of the earl's courtship to pay any mind to Hannah's comings and goings. Clearly, Charlotte was unhappy. She no doubt had expected an offer by now, but apparently had not received one.

Lord Strickland appeared to be deliberately avoiding Hannah, though why that should be Hannah had no idea. More than likely, it was her own overactive imagination that gave a different interpretation to the earl's disinterest.

The only person who commented upon her behavior was Major Prescott. More than once he had asked if she was feeling well. "You look a bit down pin," he had said to her during supper two evenings after the ball. "Are you quite well, Hannah?"

"Yes, Major, I am quite well," she had replied, and proceeded to give the first excuse that came to mind. "I am simply distracted by my studies at St. Biddulph's. There is something most puzzling about that ambulatory that has absorbed all my attention, I fear."

His interest always flagged when she mentioned the church and her explorations, so she changed the subject and asked about Miss Wetherby.

"It looks to me as though you have made progress with her, Major. It is high time you stopped flirting with me. You will never make her jealous, you know."

"My dear Hannah," he replied, "I flirt with you because you are an enchanting and delightful young woman and deserve to be flirted with, not to make Rachel jealous. But you are correct. We have come to terms with the past. Now, I am only hoping she will want to make a future together."

"Oh, Major Prescott! That is good news. Have you made her an offer yet?"

"No, but I am hoping to do so very soon. I only want to give her a bit more time to believe in me again."

"I am sure everything will work out for you, Major."

Hannah caught sight of the earl speaking with Charlotte. "I hope you will excuse me, sir, but I really would like to consult my notes on St. Biddulph's."

"Good night to you, then," he said. "I hope you solve your puzzle soon. We see far too little of you these days, Hannah my girl."

The days were easiest, when she could escape to St. Biddulph's. Each morning when she walked into the village she would see the old church, lifting its splendid Saxon tower to the sky, and her spirits rose. She dragged her thoughts from the earl and her stupid infatuation and concentrated on the architecture and its mysteries. She gave herself over to it, and allowed it to perform its familiar seduction.

The simple basilican plan, the round-headed doorways, the pointed three-light windows with plain intersecting tracery all worked together to induce a sense of peace and calm, as they were no doubt meant to do, echoing the uncomplicated faith of the converted Saxons.

It was easy enough to give in to the illusion that life was as controlled and ordered as the lines of the nave, to forget about the complication of having fallen in love with the man her sister was to marry.

Hannah allowed herself to be consumed with a detailed examination of the apse and the sunken ambulatory, determined to discover whether or not a crypt had once existed. The ambulatory was original to the seventh-century structure. The apse had been rebuilt in the fifteenth century, and probably at least one other time previous to that. Hannah studied each wall, each window, each arch, each doorway, even the stones in the floor in an effort to determine the original design.

She left Epping early each morning and returned briefly in the early afternoon for luncheon. She made the short trip back to the church in the afternoon, often remaining until the sun set. Hannah's long absences from the hall meant that she spent less time with the children, and little Amy complained that she was ignoring them. When Hannah explained that she was looking for a hidden room at the church, Amy invited herself along.

It soon became routine that during Hannah's afternoon return to St. Biddulph's, Amy accompanied her. She did not mind, really. The child was not the sort who peppered one with constant questions. She seemed to understand the seriousness of Hannah's work, and watched quietly. Sometimes she fell asleep on a bench, but most times she watched with a child's fascination for secret rooms and hidden treasure.

On the fourth afternoon that Amy accompanied her, they were joined by Charles and Henry. Intrigued by Amy's tales of a secret room, the twins wanted to see for themselves. They were met at the church by Mr. Cushing, who had been following Hannah's progress with great interest.

The rector explained that he had to be away that afternoon to visit an ailing parishioner and would not be available for their customary dish of tea. He was most anxious about her explorations, however, and asked that Hannah inform him the following morning of any progress. With a fond farewell, he left Hannah and the children alone in the old church.

The twins were disappointed that no secret passage or doorway had been discovered, and were impatient with Hannah's slow, meticulous examination of the angles of the walls in relation to the chancel arch. Soon enough, they were off investigating the effigies of twelfth- and thirteenth-century knights that lined the edges of the nave.

Hannah knelt on her hands and examined the arrangement of floor tiles in the southern part of the apse. Amy quietly knelt at her side, tracing with a pudgy finger the outline of faded trefoil patterns on the large tiles.

Amy was a beautiful little girl. Hannah supposed that Amy must constantly remind Lord Strickland of his late wife. She bore a remarkable resemblance to the portrait of her mother in the Long Gallery. Cousin Winifred had mentioned that the marriage of the earl and the late countess had been a love match, and that the earl had been devastated by his wife's death. A second marriage was necessary, Cousin Winifred had said, in order to provide a mother for his children.

How could he bear to have his beautiful children raised by another woman? Especially by Charlotte, who, Hannah suspected, did not particularly like children.

And how could any woman, even Charlotte, bear to be less than first, or even second, in Lord Strickland's heart?

Hannah forced such thoughts from her mind and concentrated on the floor tiles.

"Look, Hannah," said Amy, who had crawled a few feet away, closer toward the altar. "I think this one is loose."

Hannah moved to Amy's side and studied the tile Amy indicated. Good heavens, it *was* loose. Banking her excitement—it could mean nothing, after all—Hannah gently put pressure on first one side of the tile, then the other. After working at it for only a moment or two, the tile was completely loose.

Taking a deep breath, she used one of her drawing pencils to gently lift the tile. She grabbed hold carefully—it was large and heavy and unwieldy—and pulled it away from the floor.

Hannah gave a disappointed groan. Several inches below the present floor was another, older stone floor. No crypt. *Blast.* She was sure there had once been a crypt. She was sure of it.

She reached down to touch the older floor. With only the slightest pressure, it suddenly gave way and collapsed with a resounding rumble that echoed like an explosion in the old church.

Clouds of dirt and dust billowed up from the hole in the floor, causing Hannah and Amy to cough and sputter.

"What happened? What happened?" The twins came bounding into the apse. Hannah held out a hand to restrain them before they could trip into the hole.

She kept her mouth covered and waved away the dust. She could not yet see anything, but the sound of the collapse could mean only one thing.

"Boys," she said, "I think your cousin Amy has found my crypt."

"No fooling?"

"She did?"

"I did?"

"I cannot be sure yet," Hannah said, every bit as excited as they were, "but let's take a look."

When the dust cleared, a large hole in the second, older floor was revealed. There was no other layer of stone beneath it. Only empty blackness.

"Boys, dash outside for me, will you, and see if you can find a few rocks. Small ones will do. I want to see if we can determine how deep this is."

The twins ran off down the nave like two small terriers chasing the kitchen cat.

"Did I really help, Hannah?" Amy asked. "Did I help find what you were looking for?"

"Help? Sweetheart, you did more than help. You found it!" She hugged the little girl close. "What a clever girl you are, Amy, to have noticed that loose tile."

Henry and Charles were back in an instant, their hands cradling a collection of every size and shape of rock. They placed them next to Hannah, keeping one or two for themselves, and went to stand on the opposite side of the hole for better vantage.

"Now, be very quiet, everyone," Hannah said, "and listen." She picked up a rock, held it over the hole, and dropped it. In no more than the length of one breath, it clattered against something solid. A second rock afforded the same result.

"It's not as deep as a well, to be sure," she said. "But deep enough to indicate a chamber of some kind. And its floor is not dirt but something hard. Probably stone or more tile. Children, I do believe we have found ourselves a crypt."

The boys sent up a cheer, and Amy bounced on her knees with excitement.

Hannah wanted to shout, she wanted to shriek, she wanted to jump up and down for joy. She had found her crypt, a rare Saxon crypt lost for centuries beneath the double floor of the apse. It was too wonderful. It was fabulous. It was the happiest moment of her life.

And in the next instant, everything changed.

The tile Amy bounced upon became loose and collapsed beneath her. The child screamed and began to fall. Hannah leaned over and grabbed her tightly, and they both went tumbling into darkness.

Miles had spent the afternoon with his steward, inspecting the planting of new wheat. He had just returned to the stables when he saw Henry and Charles running as fast as they could across the Palladian bridge. What were those two little hellions up to now?

"Uncle Miles! Uncle Miles!"

He reined in and held his horse in place while the twins rushed toward him, arms waving frantically, eyes wild with some kind of excitement.

"Slow down, you two," he said. "What's all this commotion?"

The boys had been running so fast that when they

came to a halt they almost toppled over, then both began talking at once.

"Amy and Hannah—"

"—fell in the hole—"

"—at the church—"

"—trapped in the secret room—"

"—can't get out—"

"—and Mr. Cushing was gone and—"

"Amy's crying—"

"—they're all alone in the dark and—"

"Hannah said to send for help—"

What on earth? Sudden panic threw a rush of bile into Miles's mouth. An accident? Amy was hurt? Oh God. Oh God. Oh God.

"Quiet! Both of you! I cannot understand when you both speak at once. Charlie, there was an accident at the church?"

"Yes, Uncle Miles, that's what we've been—"

Miles raised a hand for quiet. "Is anyone hurt?" He looked at Henry.

"I don't know. Hannah said she was all right, but Amy was crying awful hard."

"Charlie, tell me what happened."

"Amy found a loose tile and then there was big boom like thunder and there was this big hole in the floor and we threw rocks in and Hannah said it was the crypt place and then the floor under Amy got loose and she started to fall and Hannah grabbed her and they both fell in!"

Good God. Amy was trapped in all that darkness beneath the floor of the church. She would be terrified—and possibly injured.

"Thank you both for running for help," he said as he turned his horse in the direction of the bridge. "I'll go to them now."

"Can we come, too?"

"No! You two stay here at the hall. It could be dangerous at the church. I don't want anyone else hurt."

With that, he spurred his mount toward the bridge and into the village.

My poor Amy, my poor little Amy.

Panic had settled in his throat. *Please heaven, let her be all right.* He couldn't bear to think of her being hurt and scared. He could not get to her fast enough.

When he reached St. Biddulph's, Miles quickly dismounted, tied the lead rope to a high branch on a nearby tree, and ran into the church.

He stood in the doorway and realized he'd forgotten to ask where the hole was. He walked through the nave, looking right and left. Where was the hole? *Think, man.* Something about a crypt. Yes, the crypt. Hannah had believed the sunken ambulatory had once surrounded a crypt. Under the apse.

He ran through the presbytery and up the steps to the apse. Then he heard the sound. *Singing?*

The muted refrain of a nursery song seemed to be coming out of nowhere. He followed the sound toward the altar.

And saw the hole.

"Amy? Amy, it's Papa. Are you all right?"

The singing stopped.

"Papa?" The tiny voice was barely audible.

"Lord Strickland? It's Hannah. Amy is here with me. We had quite a tumble, and I think she cut her leg but is otherwise unhurt. Can you help us get out?"

"I will certainly try."

"Papa!" Amy began to cry. "Papa, I want to get out of here!"

"I know, poppet. I'll get you out, do not worry."

He tested the floor tiles surrounding the hole. One side appeared precarious, but the other side seemed perfectly sound. He knelt down and bent toward the opening. As his eyes became accustomed to the dark-

ness below, he could just make out the form of Hannah
in a light-colored dress, a ghostly figure in the dark.
She appeared to be holding Amy on her lap and leaning against something large.

"Are you hurt, Hannah?"

"No, my lord. A bit bruised, perhaps, but unharmed."

"Do you think you can lift Amy up to me?"

Hannah shifted, and it appeared that she stood up.
"I think if I stand on this . . . this structure . . . I might
be able to reach you."

One end of a large rectangular shape was visible
from above. It was likely a tomb. Bless Hannah for not
scaring Amy by letting her know what sort of place
she was in. If Hannah could stand on the edge of the
tomb nearest the opening above, she just might be able
to hand Amy up to him.

He listened as Hannah first consoled Amy and told
her all was well now that her papa was here. She must
be brave and help him to get her out of the secret
room. She lifted Amy up onto the tomb, then climbed
up herself. She struggled to her feet, then she reached
an arm up toward the opening.

"If you bend down, can you reach me, my lord?"

Miles took off his coat and tossed it aside. He
stretched out flat on the floor and hung his upper body
over the secure side of the opening. He reached down
and easily clasped Hannah's hand.

Thank God. It was going to work.

She let go and bent to lift Amy into her arms. "It's all
right, Amy. Your papa is going to pull you to safety.
Now, lift your arms high while I hold you up."

Miles pulled Amy to safety, then sat back and held
her against him. She was safe. Thank heaven, she was
safe. "Amy, Amy girl," he crooned as she sobbed
against his shoulder. "Papa's here. Papa has you safe
and sound."

He never wanted to let her go, he had been so frightened for her. He held her and held her while she cried. Finally, he settled her on one knee while he examined her. Her white muslin dress was stained red along one side. He found an ugly-looking cut on her leg, and Amy wailed in pain when he gently touched it.

"Poor girl," he said. "That is a nasty cut. I'll take you right home, and we'll have Mrs. Lindquist make a bandage for you. But first, let me help Hannah."

He tried to pull Amy away, but she held on to his neck more tightly and sobbed. "Don't leave me, Papa!"

"I won't leave you, poppet, but you must let go of me so I can help Hannah."

"No!" Amy wailed.

"It won't take but a moment, sweetheart."

"No! Don't leave me!" She sobbed and held tighter. "Don't leave me!"

The poor child was hysterical. She probably had been scared to death down in the inky darkness of the crypt, not to mention the initial fright of falling. Now that she was safe, she was not going to let go of him.

"Hannah, I'm sorry, but Amy is so frightened. Will you be all right if I take her home and come back for you."

"I'll be perfectly fine, my lord. Take care of Amy." He heard a soft chuckle. "I will still be here when you return."

"Bless you, Hannah. I'll come back as quickly as I can, I promise."

"Take your time, my lord. I am perfectly content. After all, I have found my crypt!"

Chapter 13

Miles held Amy close against his chest as he rode back to Epping Hall. She had grown so much lately that taking her up with him on his horse was neither comfortable nor particularly safe. But the poor child was still trembling from the aftershock of her frightening experience and held on to him as though she never intended to let go.

Once outdoors in the sunlight, he had taken a closer look at the cut on her leg. It had bled badly, but was so covered in dirt from the fall that Miles could not determine how deep it was. Amy had had enough shocks for one day. How would she bear it if she had to have her leg stitched as well? He would need to stay by her side the whole time. He would not leave her.

But what about Hannah?

When they reached the stables, Amy would not allow herself to be handed down to a groom. She held on tight while Miles dismounted awkwardly. He gave instructions to have one of the grooms ride into the village for the doctor. Shifting Amy's weight on his hip, he carried her toward the hall.

George was passing through the entry hall, dressed for riding.

"Oh, I say, Miles, are you—"

"George! Thank heaven you're here. Amy's been injured, and—"

"Good God! What's happened?"

"There was an accident at the church," Miles said in a rush, anxious to get Amy upstairs. "Hannah is still trapped there. She is unharmed, but needs help. I had to rush Amy home and leave Hannah there alone. Can you go to her, George?"

"Yes, of course. I'll go right now."

"Thanks, old chap. I'm most grateful to you. I told Hannah I'd be right back for her, but I don't wish to leave Amy just yet."

"No," Amy whimpered, her face buried against his shoulder. "Don't go, Papa. Don't leave me."

"I won't go, poppet. Uncle George will see to Hannah, and I will stay with you." He flashed his brother a look of gratitude. "She's had quite a scare, poor thing. Let me take her upstairs."

"Do you think Hannah can walk? She told me once she wasn't much good at riding, and I believe Win took the gig to go visiting. I'd hate to put your curricle to it for such a short trip if you think she's up to walking."

Miles remembered Hannah scrambling to climb up on the tomb. "Yes, I believe she can walk. Just get her out of that hole. But I must hurry now. Thank you, George."

Miles rushed up the Grand Staircase, then up one more flight to the second floor, where the bedchambers were located. "Mrs. Lindquist!" he called out as he ran toward the nursery at the end of the corridor.

Poor old Miles, George thought as he hurried along the main drive toward the gatehouse. His brother's face had been drained of all color, obviously as shaken as Amy by whatever had happened. No doubt he was thinking of Amelia and frightened at even the remote possibility of losing someone else he loved.

Thankfully, Amy had appeared to be more scared than hurt. George wondered what exactly had happened, but he couldn't have asked Miles for the details; he was too concerned for his daughter.

He would hear the whole story from Hannah. Thank goodness she hadn't been hurt as well. *Just get her out of that hole.* What the devil did that mean? Leave it to Hannah to trip and fall into a hole. He remembered her telling him on their first meeting, when she had tripped over something or other, that her mind was usually in the clouds and not on her feet. Since she was at St. Bidd's, he could be fairly certain her attention had been nowhere near her feet.

What a delightful bumbler she was. This should prove most interesting.

As he approached the Palladian bridge—the scene of that first inauspicious encounter with Hannah—he saw Joseph and Rachel Wetherby strolling across from the other side. Rachel saw him and smiled.

The sight of her caused his heart to pound like a drummer calling troops to assemble. When she smiled like that, she looked so beautiful she almost took his breath away.

Even as a child she'd been pretty, so fair and delicate. She had not changed much in seven years, except that she had lost some of the softness of youth. She had become elegantly slender. The more prominent cheekbones gave her a patrician quality. She carried herself with grace and ease. She had grown up.

And she was beautiful.

He met them in the center of the bridge. "Good afternoon Rachel, Joseph. I looked for you earlier," he said to Rachel. "I hoped you might take a stroll with me in the gardens. We must take advantage of these last few good days of autumn before the rains begin in earnest."

"Joseph and I went to visit Mrs. Jennings in the village," Rachel said. "She does so love to entertain visitors. I think she gets lonely, and I try to stop by at least once a week to say hello."

"You are a kind-hearted creature, Rachel," George said. "As I recall, the old woman can talk for hours without taking a breath."

Joseph gave a bark of laughter. "Indeed, she does," he said. "I sometimes find myself nodding off. Rachel does a much better job at looking interested and saying all the right things. But she was very kind to us all as children, as you know. It is the least we can do to listen to her chatter and gossip now and then. Or so Rachel frequently reminds me."

"You must be tired then," George said with unfeigned disappointment. He had hoped to have another hour or so alone with her. He was doing everything possible to show her that he was not the same arrogant youth who'd betrayed her seven years ago. He wanted her to trust him again. Before he could make her an offer of marriage, he needed to be sure the past would not hang over them like a pall for the rest of their lives.

Rachel smiled and said, "Not too tired to take a stroll through the gardens."

"Would you? Excellent! Joseph, old fellow, I hope you will excuse us?"

Joseph grinned and patted his sister's hand indulgently. "It would be my pleasure. I think I shall escape to the hall and have a nap."

George took Rachel's hand, placed a fulsome kiss upon her fingers, then tucked it into the crook of his arm. It was one of those little moments of sublime contentment, with the woman he had loved all his life at his side and gazing up at him with an expression he would swear was as ardent as his own.

The three of them walked across the bridge together, through the gatehouse and past the stables. George had covered Rachel's hand with his own and kept her

pulled closer against him than was absolutely proper.
Joseph pretended not to notice. Surely he would have
given some word or sign if he had objected. It felt so
natural to be walking with Rachel like this, and with
her brother, as though seven years had not passed.
When they reached the path that led to the south gardens, they parted to go their separate ways.

It was at that moment George remembered Hannah.

"Good God!" he exclaimed. He came to an abrupt
halt, causing Rachel to stumble slightly. "I'd almost
forgot!"

Joseph, who'd walked toward the hall, turned
around and quirked a brow. "What's that, lad?"

"It's Hannah." George noticed the merest stiffening
of Rachel's hand on his arm. Surely she did not still believe him to have an interest in Hannah? Damn. "I'm
supposed to fetch her from St. Bidd's. Some sort of
minor mishap or something. You know Hannah." He
watched Rachel to gauge her reaction, but she kept her
eyes cast down.

Damn and blast. He had been making such progress
with her. He must not give her any reason to doubt
him. She might never understand if he abandoned her
for Hannah just now.

"I say, Joseph, I know it is a lot to ask, but"—he
slanted a glance toward Rachel—"would you mind
very much postponing your nap for a while and collecting Hannah for me?"

Joseph glared at him for a moment as though weigh-
ing the disadvantages of sacrificing forty winks.
"Well . . ." He sighed and cast his eyes heavenward.
"At St. Bidd's, is she?"

George nodded.

"All the way back into the village? Hmm . . ."

George began to fear that this opportunity to be
alone with Rachel, to reassure her that he had no in-

terest in Hannah, would be missed after all. Joseph was going to be difficult.

And then he saw Joseph look over at Rachel and wink. George expelled a pent-up breath in a long sigh.

"Don't look so hangdog, old boy," Joseph said, his face splitting into a grin. "You go on with Rachel. I'll see to Hannah. Don't worry about me trudging all the way to the village and back again. Good for me, eh? Nothing else to do. But afterward, I will have my nap!"

With that, he gave a wave and headed back the way they'd come, whistling an old tavern song as he sauntered along.

George looked down at Rachel and smiled. "Shall we?"

She returned his smile with a dazzling one of her own, and they made their way into the privacy of the formal gardens.

Joseph Wetherby found himself quite pleased with the way things were looking between his sister and George Prescott. Those two had been destined for one another since they were children. It had been a damned foolish situation that drove them apart. If young Prescott hadn't bolted for the Peninsula, Joseph might have been tempted to beat him to a pulp at the very least.

He had not blamed Rachel for never wanting to set eyes on the young cur again. Walking in on something like that would have been shocking to any gently bred, innocent girl. But when the man she loved was involved, how much more devastating it must have been. When Prescott left for the army, Joseph had assumed that was the end of it, and that Rachel would get on with her life.

She had mourned the loss of her love as would be expected. She even seemed to have gotten over it after a time. She was only eighteen years old, young enough to bounce back, to find another love.

But she never had. Rachel had never again shown any interest in a Season or the Marriage Mart or courtship. It was as though she had decided she could love only once, and when that had failed, there was no second chance. She kept to the house, seldom going beyond Northamptonshire, and appeared to settle into an early spinsterhood. She never mentioned Prescott or asked Miles about him, but Joseph had often wondered if she waited for his eventual return.

Concerned for her, he had been imprudent enough to ask some years ago if she was indeed keeping herself available for Prescott. She had been so furious at him for presuming to ask such a question, she hadn't spoken to him for a week. He never mentioned it again.

It was beginning to look as if he'd been right all along. He was glad for it. Rachel wasn't meant to be a spinster.

As he passed the stables, he saw Lord Tyndall approaching from the eastern woodlands. A gun was slung over one shoulder, and he carried a heavy sack. It was clear what old Godfrey had been up to this afternoon.

"Afternoon, Tyndall," he said. "Good shooting today?"

"Capital, Wetherby. Capital." He held out his sack like a trophy. "Every grouse as plump as a Christmas goose."

"One of these afternoons I shall have to join you," Joseph said. "My own park is well stocked this year. Once you've stripped poor old Miles of every bird, we can stray onto my land and have a go, eh?"

"Oh, I say, that reminds me," Godfrey said. "I did stray a bit far afield today. To the edge of your land, in fact. Saw a section of wattle down in your northern field."

"The devil!"

"Yes, out near the upland pasture. You know the place I mean?"

"I do, confound it," Joseph said. He removed his hat and slapped it angrily against his thigh. "And if the wattle is down, there's sure to be some blasted sheep that find it and wander through."

"Just what I thought. Figured you'd want to know."

"Blast it all! I knew I should have planted double oxer. I'd better go see to it before my sheep begin trampling Miles's wheat seed. He'll have my head if his fields are ruined. Much obliged to you for the warning, Tyndall."

"Any time. Good luck to you."

"Oh, hell and damnation," Joseph exclaimed. He stomped the ground so hard a tiny cloud of dust rose from his boot. "I almost forgot. Tyndall, I have promised to fetch Hannah Fairbanks from the church in the village. Was on my way there just now. I don't suppose I could prevail upon you to go in my place? I really must see to that wattle, but I can't leave the poor girl stranded."

"The church in the village? The one she's always poking about in?"

"Yes. She's there now."

"Well, of course I'll fetch her for you," Godfrey said. "Happy to do it. Very fond of the girl, don't you know. You see to your sheep, and I'll go for Hannah."

Joseph clapped Godfrey soundly on the back. "I am in your debt, Tyndall. Much obliged."

Joseph doubled back to the stables, had his horse saddled within moments, and rode out to inspect the damaged fence.

Godfrey began to walk toward the hall. He would change out of his shooting clothes and clean up a bit before going into the village to escort Hannah back. He did not like to offer his arm to a young lady, even a ramshackle one like Hannah, while covered in dirt and blood, and toting a gun.

Just then he looked up to see the distinctive plump silhouette of a ruffed grouse soar overhead. It was followed by several others. They dipped out of sight in the woodlands to the east.

It was very tempting. He looked down at his sack and pondered the situation. It had been a good day, but he'd had better. He might be able to fill the sack with one more pass through the woods.

He would take only a half hour or so. An hour at most. There would still be plenty of time to fetch Hannah, would there not? She liked nothing better than to nose around old churches. She wouldn't mind waiting a bit longer, would she? Probably would not even notice if he was a bit late.

Another grouse flew overhead and settled the question. Godfrey hefted his gun onto his shoulder and turned toward the woods.

Chapter 14

Miles wandered into the blue salon and sank wearily into a chair opposite the one occupied by his sister. Winifred looked up from her needlework.

"Is she going to be all right?" she asked.

Miles sighed and offered a smile. "Yes. It was hardly more than a scratch, thank God, not deep at all. Dr. Abernathy gave her a nice big bandage that should make her feel very important for a few days. Mrs. Lindquist tucked her into bed and she fell right to sleep."

"That is good news," Winifred said. "I know how worried you were."

"I don't mind telling you I was scared almost to death. You ought to have seen the blood on her dress." He leaned his head against the back of the chair and blew his breath out through puffed cheeks. "I think my heart has only just now begun to beat normally. I believe I could use a brandy."

He stood up, stretched, and walked to the sideboard, where several decanters and glasses were arranged on a silver tray. "Something for you, Win?"

"Nothing so strong as that," she said. "But I admit a dish of tea would not be amiss."

After he'd poured himself a brandy and rung for tea, Winifred said to him, "You must get used to these things, Miles. Children will have their little accidents. You should try raising two fearless boys. If I were to fret over every scrape and bruise as you do, I would not have a single dark hair left in my head."

"I don't mean to fuss over them," Miles said, "but they are so precious to me. And it has been especially difficult for Amy these last two years. I cannot help feeling overprotective, I suppose."

"All is well in any case," Winifred said. "The boys, by the way, are all agog over this secret room of Hannah's. Where is the girl? She must be positively beside herself over the discovery."

"Indeed she must. But I haven't seen her since I returned from the church. Perhaps we should all take a tour tomorrow and see what she has found. Ah, here are George and Rachel." He lowered his voice to a conspiratorial whisper. "And looking as starry-eyed as two adolescents."

"Hullo, Miles, Win." George entered the salon and led Rachel to a sofa. "A bit early for brandy, ain't it? How is Amy?"

"She is quite well," Miles replied. "No serious injury at all. Her father, on the other hand, is still recovering." He held up his glass and cocked his head in its direction. "Our sister prefers tea. Will you join us?"

A footman came into the room in answer to the bell, and Miles asked for a pot of tea to be brought up. George sat on the sofa next to Rachel, not quite touching but within easy reach. He did not seem to be able to take his eyes off her. Rachel had a flushed look about her. Miles would guess that she had recently been very thoroughly kissed.

"Did you have any trouble rescuing Hannah from that great hole?" Miles asked.

"Oh, well, as to that," George said, "I didn't actually go after her."

"What?" Miles bolted upright. "Do you mean to tell me she is still—"

George raised a hand. "Hold on, old man. No need to fly into the boughs. I asked Joseph to fetch her."

"Joseph? But I haven't seen him all day."

"He was out with Rachel. I met them on my way to St. Bidd's. But it was such a beautiful day and"—he smiled at Rachel—"I could never resist a beautiful woman. We went for a stroll through the gardens, and Joseph went on to St. Bidd's to rescue Hannah."

"I hope she is all right," Miles said, worried that she had been forced to remain in the dark crypt all alone.

"What is this great hole anyway?" George asked.

"Apparently she discovered an old crypt beneath the floor of the church. A portion of the old floor collapsed. Hannah and Amy fell in."

"Good heavens!" Rachel exclaimed.

"So that's how Amy got hurt," George said. "Thank God it was nothing serious." After a moment, he began to chuckle softly. "And you left Hannah trapped in the crypt?"

"She was unhurt," Miles said. "She scrambled easily enough onto a sarcophagus to lift Amy up to me." As serious as it might have been, the whole incident was very Hannah-like. He tried not to smile, but failed.

George burst into laughter. "Ha! I can just see it. Hannah perched in the dark on an old tomb. She probably never enjoyed herself more."

They were all four chuckling when the butler and a maid arrived with tea. The service was set before Winifred, who poured for the rest of them, except for Miles, who still nursed his brandy.

"Moffit, would you send a message to Miss Fairbanks inviting her to join us for tea?"

"Right away, my lord."

"Excuse me, my lord," the maid said.

"What is it, Bessie?"

"So far as I knows, my lord," she said, keeping her eyes downcast in the most deferential manner, "Miss

Fairbanks hadn't never come back from the village yet."

"Are you certain?" Miles said. "She was with Mr. Wetherby."

"Mr. Wetherby," said Moffit, "has not yet returned to the hall, my lord. I am told he took his horse and rode to his own estate on a matter of some urgency."

A twinge of uneasiness crept up Miles's spine. "I don't understand," he said. "George, are you certain he agreed to go help Hannah? Had he already returned from his estate when you saw him?"

"He could not have," Rachel said. "He and I had been in the village, visiting Mrs. Jennings. Then we met up with George, and Joseph agreed to go to the church. But that was some time ago."

"Good Lord," Miles said. "You don't imagine Hannah is still . . . still in that hole, do you?"

"Hullo! Hullo!" The boisterous greeting came from Godfrey, who marched into the salon at that moment along with Charlotte. He was grinning and strutting like a rooster. "My dear." He went to Winifred's side and bent to kiss her cheek. "What a day I have had. What a day, what a day! Fourteen grouse. Would you believe it, Win? Fourteen!"

"How nice, dear," Winifred said. "But don't you look like five pence. Are you going out?"

Charlotte took a seat near the earl and gave him a flirtatious smile.

"Only to the church," Godfrey said. "Supposed to escort Hannah back to the hall."

"What!" Miles and George exclaimed in unison.

"But I sent Joseph to fetch her," George said.

"He had a problem with a wattle fence and dashed on home for a spell. Told him I'd collect the girl myself."

"But that was almost two hours ago," George said.

"I went back in for one last shoot," Godfrey replied. "Found a nice little covey and—"

"You went back for more shooting instead of going to Hannah?" Miles felt like a teakettle ready to boil.

"Just for a short while," Godfrey replied, obviously puzzled by Miles's agitation. "Then came back to clean up a bit. Didn't want to escort the girl in all my dirt, did I?"

"Escort her?" Miles's voice rose almost to a shout. "Escort her? The poor girl is trapped beneath a collapsed floor. She doesn't need escorting. She needs rescuing!"

Charlotte went pale and clapped a hand to her mouth.

Godfrey looked at Miles blankly. "What's this you say? Trapped? Nobody said anything about her being trapped. Wetherby simply said to fetch her back to the hall. Good God." He ran a hand through his hair, looking thoroughly chagrined. "Good God. I had no idea. I'll go for her at once."

"*I'll* go for her," Miles announced. "The rest of you obviously cannot be trusted. That poor girl. George, I blame you for this. I counted on you. I had promised Hannah to return for her right away, but you saw how frightened Amy was. You know I could not leave her. I depended on you to honor my promise to Hannah."

"I'm sorry, Miles."

"Don't apologize go me. Apologize to Hannah when she returns for leaving her alone and stranded."

"My lord?" Charlotte's voice was not the usual seductive whisper, but thin and strangled. Her hands clutched at the arms of her chair. "Is Hannah . . . is she injured? Is she going to be all right?"

Miles went to her and touched her hand lightly. "She was uninjured when I brought Amy home. Please do not worry. I am angry because she has been trapped in a dark, moldy, ancient crypt for more than two hours without anyone to help her out. It's inexcusable. But I'll go to her now and bring her back myself. Do not worry, Charlotte. She will be fine."

"Thank you, my lord."

With a scowl at George, Miles left the salon and made his way to the stables. He took the gig, figuring Hannah would be too exhausted after her ordeal to walk even the short distance to the hall.

Though he assumed she was probably safe and unharmed, it galled him that he had let her down and caused her to have to stay in that awful place for so long. He cursed himself for not pulling her out when he had the chance. If only Amy hadn't been so upset, and if only he'd known her injuries were so minor, he would have taken the time to get Hannah out of there.

If anything had happened to her, it was all his fault. He would never forgive himself. But even if she was safe, she was all alone in the dark, no doubt wondering why the devil no one had come to help her, believing herself abandoned. She must be frightened after all this time. And cold. Poor Hannah. Poor dear Hannah.

Once over the Palladian bridge, Miles flicked the reins, hoping to encourage a bit more speed out of the horse. He was desperate to get to the church. She had been trapped for too long. He had to get to her. His mind reeled with images of Hannah at the ball, those great blue eyes that gazed up at him, brimming with tears.

Was she anxious and scared now? Would he need to take her in his arms again to comfort her?

Poor Hannah. Poor, sweet, adorable Hannah.

Hannah ran her hands carefully and slowly along the cold stone of the western wall. At least she thought it was the western wall. She had become a bit disoriented during her blind exploration of the crypt. She halted when the wall dropped off and became set back into an alcove or niche of some kind. It was the first such niche she had found and she could not quell the rush of excitement that caused her heart to beat rapidly. Could this be what she hoped it was?

She slowly followed the lower edge of the niche with her hand. The edge was at about waist height and it was not more than half a meter in width—too small for a statue. Besides, the Saxons did not much go in for statues in their churches. She gingerly reached into the niche and immediately encountered something solid. Square. Wooden. A small coffer? For a moment her fingers got tangled up in a mass of cobwebs. Wrinkling her nose in distaste at the sticky wisps, she brushed them away as best she could and cautiously examined the coffer. Her fingers came upon a metal lid—gold?— with some sort of design in heavy relief. In the center was a finial topped with a cross.

This had to be it! A reliquary of St. Biddulph. Every early Saxon church had some sort of relic of its patron saint. Mr. Cushing had said that no such relic had been found here. This had to be it. The ambulatory may have originally been built to surround the reliquary and its shrine. And Hannah thought she may well be the first person to lay eyes on it—or at least hands—in over a thousand years!

She gave out a whoop and did a little dance on the uneven stone floor. Miss Hannah Fairbanks of Dudley-on-the-Meese had made a great discovery. She wanted to shout. She wanted to sing. She wanted to *tell* someone!

Hannah had never been so excited in her entire life.

She ran her hand along the edge of the coffer to the back, and began to feel around to see if there were any other objects in the niche.

"Hannah! Hannah!" The sound of heavy footsteps came from above.

Blast. Already?

"Hannah, you poor girl! Are you all right?"

She moved to stand next to the tomb beneath the opening. The earl's face looked down from above. Though the light was dim, she could not mistake the expression of concern.

"Yes, my lord," she said. "I am perfectly all right."

"But—"

"In fact, I have never been better in all my life. My lord, you cannot imagine all the wonderful things I have found." Finally, someone to talk to! "I have made the most wonderful discovery! It is a true Saxon crypt, hidden for heaven only knows how many centuries. There are several large stone sarcophagi and tomb slabs with very distinctive Saxon decoration. I could feel the designs with my fingers, they are unmistakable. And there are low slabs with reclining effigies that are older than anything upstairs but still probably Norman."

"But, Hannah—"

"And the reliquary! There is a niche with a coffer that I am certain is a reliquary. And if it is, it probably contains some relic of St. Biddulph. It has—"

"Hannah! I have come to get you out of there. Let me help you up, and then you may tell me all about it."

"Oh." She looked around her in the dark, thinking of all the marvels she'd uncovered. "I had hoped to have a bit more time," she said. "I did not expect you back so soon."

"So soon . . ." He paused, and then all at once the crypt echoed with the earl's laughter. It surrounded her, enfolded her, filling the dank, heavy air that had until now been silent as . . . as a tomb. She had never known him to laugh like that.

"Hannah," he said at last, his voice still quivering with amusement, "don't you want to come out?"

"Well . . ." She considered the matter. "If you could

send down a few candles and the occasional piece of bread, I should think I could stay down here for several days. Oh, and paper, too. And pencils."

He began laughing again. "Hannah, Hannah," he said. "I have come all contrite for having left you so long, worried that you were alone and frightened. And here you are, not ready to be rescued at all!"

"Oh." Even in the dim light she could see the laughter dancing in his eyes. "I did not realize I needed to be rescued." His laughter had become infectious, and she found herself grinning up at him. "But I suppose I cannot stay here forever, can I?"

"No, I think not."

"I can always come back tomorrow, can I not? With candles?"

"Indeed you can," he said, still chuckling. "Now, get up on that tomb and let me pull you out."

Hannah glanced around the crypt wistfully. She supposed it would still be here tomorrow. After climbing up onto the lid of the sarcophagus, silently apologizing to its occupant for her impertinence, she looked up to the opening.

As he had done with Amy, the earl stretched out flat on the floor above and reached his hands down for her. In all the time she had spent exploring the dark crypt, she had not considered how she might get out. Suddenly, it looked nearly impossible.

"Are you sure this will work, my lord? After all, I am not as small as Amy."

Another chuckle from above. "Have you no confidence in my strength, Miss Fairbanks? You wound me."

"It's just that . . . Oh, well. I suppose it is worth a try."

She lifted her arms above her head, ignoring the distinct sound of a seam ripping at her sleeve, and easily reached his hands. That was the simple part.

His hands slid down and clasped her forearms in a strong grip. "Hold on to my arms, Hannah." She did. He had removed his coat and rolled up his sleeves so that she grasped bare skin. Why that should discompose her so, she did not know.

"Ready?"

"As I'll ever be."

He gave a great tug. Hannah closed her eyes tight when her feet left the ground. One more tug and she was soaring upward and bouncing along the ragged edge of the opening. She gave a little gasp, and he pulled her awkwardly onto the floor of the chancel.

They both lay panting on the floor, still grasping one another's arms. Well, this is typical, Hannah thought. Here she was splayed out like a dead chicken again, this time taking the earl down with her. Recalling the night of the ball, she wondered how many more times she was destined to make a fool of herself in front of this man. She ought to have been mortified. She ought to have wanted to die. Instead, she began to laugh. And laugh. She laughed until her whole body shook with it. Then she noticed the earl was laughing, too. The two of them lay spraddled on the floor, cackling like idiots.

Whenever one of them looked over to the other, they laughed harder. They could not speak for laughing.

Finally, the earl scrambled to his knees, pulling Hannah up with him. They continued to hold on to each other, and continued to laugh.

Hannah looked into his eyes, still brimming with mirth, and fell in love all over again. Wildly, desperately, absurdly in love.

The look in his eyes changed, and she realized their laughter had subsided. He reached out and wiped a thumb across her cheek. She was no doubt covered in dirt. What a sight she must be.

"You make it difficult to be a hero, Hannah."

The intense look in his eyes made her feel odd and prickly all over, the way she had felt at the ball when she had thought he was going to kiss her. "And yet," she said, her voice unsteady, "you always seem to be rescuing me."

He touched her hair very lightly and smiled. "But you are not the typical damsel in distress, are you? Not this time, anyway. You would rather I'd let you stay in that dank old crypt."

"But you should see what is down there!" she said, her excitement renewed at the very thought of it. "It's an honest-to-God Saxon crypt. And I wouldn't be surprised if it had originally been a Roman cellar. Can you imagine? I found what felt like a carving of an eagle on one wall that felt very Roman. Actually Roman! One of the arches seems to be constructed of thin Roman bricks, but I couldn't reach it enough to be sure."

"Hannah—"

"Up here you can see the chancel was rebuilt for the first time probably in the tenth century. But I am willing to swear the crypt walls are seventh century. Eighth century at the latest. And the effigies are marvelous!"

"Hannah—"

"And the reliquary! My heavens, it feels as if it might be gold, and it probably contains—"

He stopped her words with his mouth.

Good Lord. He was kissing her. He was really kissing her this time.

She had never before been kissed. It was not at all what she expected. His lips did not stay pressed against hers, but moved gently over her mouth—tasting, exploring, tantalizing. It was wonderful.

She gave a little moan, closed her eyes, and surrendered to the pure sensation of it.

He pulled her closer. One hand held the back of her head, fingers threaded through her hair. His other arm wrapped her tightly about the waist. Hannah's arms had somehow snaked around his neck and shoulders. Their bodies pressed close together, with only the thin muslin of her dress and the lawn of his shirt between them.

Though Hannah focused on the magic he performed with his lips, she was not unaware of the way her breasts pushed against his chest, the way his fingers dipped down to caress her neck, the way her skin seemed to tingle from the roots of her hair all the way to her toes.

It was wonderful. It was spectacular. It was exhilarating.

And it was over in less than a moment.

Chapter 15

Miles had been ready to thrust his tongue into her mouth when a sudden attack of reason overtook him. What was he doing?

Each of them was in a state of disarray, kneeling knee-to-knee with their bodies pressed together in a decidedly intimate manner. In another moment he might have made love to this young girl on the floor of a church. A church, for God's sake! What if someone had walked in? What if the rector had chosen that moment to return?

He grabbed Hannah somewhat roughly by the arms, pushed her away, and then rose to his feet. Running his hand through his hair, he looked down at her, thoroughly ashamed of himself. She sat back on her heels and stared up at him with those big, guileless eyes.

He could not bear to look at her, to see the confusion and hurt in her face. He turned away, adjusted the sleeves of his shirt, and bent to retrieve his coat.

"I am sorry, Hannah," he said. "That was unpardonable of me. I should never have done such a thing. It was a mistake. I hope you will forgive me."

"A mistake?" Her voice cracked on the word.

"Yes, a mistake. I'm so sorry, Hannah."

She sat there in silence while he pulled on his coat. He'd never felt so awkward in his life. He did not know what to say to her. He had not meant to kiss her.

Ever since the evening of the ball when he'd first recognized his attraction to her, he'd done his best to avoid her. He had no intention of acting on his foolish, imprudent desire. He thought he'd actually talked himself out of it, recollecting her youth and innocence and his intentions to avoid young girls.

But she was a singularly unconventional sort of girl—so spirited, so genuine, so completely diverting. He couldn't remember ever laughing as he had with Hannah. Not even with Amelia.

When she had begun, yet again, to chatter enthusiastically about her discovery, her face had lit up like a branch of candles. Her eyes had flashed like fervent blue fire in the dim light of the church. She was radiant beneath the dirt on her face. Dazzling with the intensity of her excitement. Enchanting. Irresistible.

Almost without conscious thought, he had reached out to her in an effort to bask in her light. He could not have stopped himself if he tried.

How could he possibly explain all that to her?

When he turned around, she looked so bewildered he almost caught her up in his arms again. Her hair tumbled about her shoulders in a riot of curls, laced here and there with cobwebs. Her face was smudged with dirt, and her dress was torn and filthy. The dank, musty smell of the crypt had seeped into her clothes and her hair. She was a mess.

She was the most adorable thing he'd ever seen.

"Have you asked Charlotte to marry you?" she asked.

The question took him so much by surprise that he flinched. "No," he said. "No, I haven't."

"But you will," she said. She rose to her knees, then more awkwardly to her feet. She looked down at her dirty dress, made a face, and then dismissed the dirt with a flick of her wrist. "You are going to marry my sister," she went on, "and yet you kissed me. You ought not to have done that, you know."

"I know, Hannah. But I'm not—"

"Do you think you can just go around kissing people without any concern for their feelings?"

"Hannah, I—"

"Do you think me such a child that I am immune to your kisses? That I would not understand? That I would not respond? Well, you were wrong, Lord Strickland."

"Hannah—"

"I am not a child. I am a woman with a woman's feelings. It was cruel of you to make me feel like that— all warm and soft inside, like jelly—when you mean to marry my sister and have no interest in me whatsoever. It is not at all what I would expect from a gentleman."

Miles reeled as if struck. He ought to have expected such a forthright response. She was not one to disguise her emotions. Even so, he felt as though he had been pummeled.

"Hannah . . . Hannah, I'm so sorry. I didn't mean to hurt you. But there are two things I want you to know."

She glared at him, but did not respond.

"I do not think of you as a child, Hannah. You are a beautiful, intelligent, and desirable woman." As he spoke the words, he suddenly realized how much he meant them. She was a woman, not a girl. He had not thought of her as a girl when he'd held her in his arms. She had been as responsive and passionate as he might have expected from someone of her uninhibited nature. He smiled with new comprehension.

Hannah was a woman.

"And I have not asked your sister to marry me," he said.

She gave a little snort as if she didn't believe him.

"Even so," she said, "I do not wish to speak with you anymore just now. You unsettle me. I am going back to Epping Hall."

"I brought the gig. Let me drive you back."

"No. I wish to be alone. Please do not follow me."

She gathered up her notebooks and retrieved the pelisse that had been tossed over a stone effigy. He reached out to help her with it, but she shook her head and turned away. "You might leave a note for Mr. Cushing, warning him of the hole," she said. "Or perhaps you can find something to cover it with. I shouldn't want anyone else to fall in."

Without waiting for a response, she turned and walked down the nave and out the front entrance.

Miles smiled at her retreating figure. Hannah was hurt and dirty and angry, and yet he smiled. He saw her with a new clarity, and his heart was full to bursting.

He had made a decision.

The early dusk of autumn had settled on the village. Candlelight flickered through cottage windows as Hannah walked down the lane from the church. She looked neither right nor left, keeping her eyes straight ahead. But not on the lane. She had no need to watch the path she had tramped back and forth upon every day for the last month and more. Her eyes focused on nothing except the effort not to cry.

It felt as though a hot ember were lodged in the back of her throat. She could not seem to swallow. Her thoughts whirled in drunken circles, first in one direction, then another. It had been the most wonderful and the most horrible day of her life.

She tried to concentrate on the crypt and the thrill of discovery. But the earl's kiss overshadowed even that.

Why had he done it? He could not possibly have a serious interest in her. Though he hadn't yet asked

Charlotte to marry him, he did not deny that he might yet make her an offer. Hannah could not understand why this strictly proper and formal gentleman would so forget himself as to kiss her.

He did not at all seem the sort of gentleman to take advantage of a woman for the sheer pleasure of doing so. She had also thought him sincere in his courtship of Charlotte and could not imagine him deliberately betraying her.

And so, what had happened? Why had he done it?

The more she thought on it, the more she began to realize it was her own fault. She had sent him sprawling in a heap on the floor. She had smeared dirt all over his fine lawn shirt. She had made him laugh. Her own antics had forced him to behave in a manner that was foreign to his nature. His kiss had been simply a consequence of uncharacteristic behavior.

It was a mistake.

That was why he had seemed so brusque and almost angry afterward. He had, of course, said all the proper words of apology and justification, but he had been angry. At her. Hannah had caused him to fall off his high horse for a moment, long enough for him to make a mistake. But it took only a moment for him to pick himself up and haul himself back up into the saddle, his usual controlled demeanor intact. A simple mistake. Nothing more.

If it was so wrong, why did it have to be so wonderful? And was it so wonderful just because kisses were, or because it had been him? Why couldn't she have hated it? Why couldn't it have been awkward and uncomfortable and distasteful?

The wretched man was making it very difficult for her not to love him, kissing her like that.

She had passed over the Palladian bridge, through the old gatehouse, and onto the gravel path leading to Epping Hall. *What shall I do? What shall I do?* The question became a litany punctuated with every crunch of gravel beneath her feet.

She should leave, that is what she should do. She should go to Bertram's.

But what about St. Biddulph's? What about the crypt?

Hannah had never faced such a quandary in her life. How could she weigh the wonders of the crypt against this very awkward situation with Lord Strickland? If she stayed to investigate the crypt fully, she would be forced into the earl's company more than she could bear. But if she left in order to avoid him, what would become of the crypt?

She wanted to scream with frustration. How could she make such a decision?

She must gather her scattered wits and decide what to do. It was much worse this time than after the almost-kiss at the ball. This time had been real. How could she pretend to forget the feel of his mouth on hers, the hint of brandy on his lips, the faint scent of leather and bay rum? How could she forget the way he'd wrapped her in his arms and pressed his body against hers?

She reached up to touch her lips. They felt different, somehow. Almost as though she could still feel him there, as though he'd left some kind of permanent imprint.

It was much, much worse this time.

Hannah decided not to make a grand entrance through the Great Hall. She must look a fright. She walked along to the western wing where she had discovered a seldom-used entry. Since her bedchamber was in this wing, it had become quite convenient to come and go by way of this entry. Thankfully, it had not yet been locked for the night. She made her way up a service stairway to the second floor and along a blessedly empty corridor to her bedchamber.

Sometime later, while she soaked in a steaming copper tub, Hannah decided the discovery at St. Biddulph's was too important to abandon. Before today, she had been fairly successful at avoiding Lord Strickland. And Charlotte. So long as no engagement was officially announced, Hannah supposed she could bear up.

The key was to work quickly. She did not know when the earl planned to make his offer. It was still three weeks until the first fox hunt of the season. Though Winifred and Godfrey planned to stay through November, Charlotte had intended to return to Dudley-on-the-Meese directly after the first hunt. She was not interested in sport, but was keen to be around for the opening-day festivities. Of course, that was before she'd met Lord Strickland and set her cap for him.

If the earl had not made an offer by then, Hannah suspected even someone as determined as Charlotte would give up and go home. But such a thing was highly unlikely. The earl would surely make an offer before then.

In the meantime, Hannah could spend her days exploring the crypt. Neither Charlotte nor the earl was likely to disturb her there. She could beg exhaustion in the evenings and take to her bed early.

But the moment an engagement was announced, she would bolt. Crypt or no crypt, she wouldn't be able to face either of them. She would go to Bertram.

Her only hope was that the earl would continue to drag his feet where Charlotte was concerned and give her more time at St. Biddulph's.

No one thought it odd that Hannah did not come down for supper that evening. The entire household knew of her two-hour ordeal in the uncovered crypt.

No one, of course, knew of what had happened between her and Miles. At least, he hoped not.

Charlotte said she had spoken with Hannah. During and after supper she had been as openly flirtatious as ever. Surely she would not have been if Hannah had blurted out something about their kiss. Had she kept her tongue between her teeth for once?

Miles knew Hannah had stayed upstairs so she wouldn't have to face him. He did not blame her. She was still convinced he was going to marry her sister. He had confused her. He had—what had she said?— made her feel all warm and soft inside. He smiled at that. He wanted to tell her she made him feel the same way. He wanted to tell her lots of things. And he would. Tomorrow.

As he walked down the corridor to the nursery wing, he marveled that he had been so blind, so stupid, so intent on one course of action.

His sole reason for considering a second marriage was to provide a mother for his daughters. Hannah had made her way into their hearts from the very first day. They loved her. Amy positively adored her. She had begun to break out of her solemn little shell, thanks to Hannah. Why, then, had it never occurred to him that Hannah would make the perfect mother for Amy and Caro?

Because he thought her too young. Because he'd convinced himself he did not want a young woman for a wife. He was thirteen years her senior. That much of an age difference still made him nervous. Yet it was fairly typical among his class. His own mother had been fifteen years younger than his father. Godfrey was ten years older than Win. Charlotte had admitted her first husband had been twenty-five years her senior. His friend the Duke of Carlisle was twelve years older than his betrothed, Catherine Forsythe.

It was his own failed courtship of Miss Forsythe that

had set Miles's mind against marriage to a woman that young. He had built up this phantom obstacle that made him blind to the true merits of Hannah as a potential wife. He had convinced himself that an older woman, a woman like Charlotte, was what he wanted.

And yet there had been no comparison between his kiss with Charlotte and his kiss with Hannah. There had been no spontaneity, no urgency, no passion when he'd kissed Charlotte. It had been expected, perfunctory. Whereas with Hannah . . .

Even though he had not taken that kiss as far as he would have liked, it had still managed to shoot a bolt of fire straight through to his vitals.

He would have to tell Amelia. Would she understand?

Miles quietly entered the bedchamber where his daughters slept, as he did every night before retiring. He bent over Caro's little bed and ran his fingers lightly over her soft dark curls. One small bare foot peeked out from under the blanket. Miles smiled and gently tucked it back under. She had been as active as a wiggly worm since she was an infant, and he often found her tangled up in her covers. He stroked her petal-soft cheek with the back of a finger. She stirred slightly but did not wake. He bent down and kissed her. "Good night, pumpkin."

When he went to Amy's bed, her eyes fluttered open and looked up at him sleepily. "Hello, poppet," he whispered. "You ought to be asleep. Does your leg hurt?"

"No. I have a bandage."

"Yes, you do. Let's take a look at it." He pulled back the covers and lifted the hem of her nightgown to examine the bandage Dr. Abernathy had fashioned that afternoon. It was rather more elaborate than necessary, but it was still in place. "You must take care that it does not come off, poppet, so that your cut will heal properly."

"Yes, Papa. Papa?"

"Hmm?"

"Did you know I helped Hannah find the secret room? She said I was very clever."

"And so you are. I'm sorry you fell, though, and had to stay down in the dark until I came to get you."

"I was kind of scared, but Hannah made me feel better. She held me on her lap and told stories and sang songs."

Miles had almost forgotten about the singing he'd heard when he had entered the chancel.

"You like Hannah a lot, don't you, poppet?"

"I love Hannah," Amy said. "She's my friend. She doesn't talk to us the way other ladies do. She talks to me and Caro like we were regular people. And she always sits down on the floor with us or puts us on her lap. She says she likes to talk eye to eye."

That she does, thought Miles.

"Hannah talks to me about Mama, too."

"She does?"

"Her mama died, too, and she still feels real sad sometimes, like me. But she made me talk about all the good things I remembered about Mama, and I didn't feel so sad anymore."

Miles gathered Amy up and held her tight. He could not speak for a moment, and rocked her quietly in his arms.

"Amy," he said at last, "how would you like to have Hannah for your new mama?"

She yawned against his shoulder. "I'd like it," she said sleepily. "Caro would, too. We'd like it a lot. She's better than that other lady. Hannah's fun and makes us laugh."

"Me, too, poppet. She makes me laugh, too. I'm going to ask her to marry me."

"I'm glad, Papa." She gave another great gaping yawn and wriggled back down onto her pillow.

"So am I," he said. "Now give me a kiss and then you should go back to sleep."

She reached up her arms and he bent down to her. She wrapped her arms around his neck and gave him a sloppy kiss on the cheek. Then she snuggled down into the covers and was asleep almost at once. Miles tucked the blankets under her chin. "Good night, poppet."

It seemed his daughters were quicker and smarter than he was. He ought to have let them pick out their own mother and saved him a great deal of time and effort.

What remained was for him to convince Hannah that he would make a good husband. He did not believe she had a very good opinion of him at the moment. Tomorrow he would set about changing her mind.

Chapter 16

The crisp bite of autumn chilled the air. Early morning sun washed the church in tones of bronze and glinted off the golden leaves of the surrounding elm trees. St. Biddulph's tower rose proudly, beckoning Hannah to the wonders inside.

She carried notebooks, sketch pads, pencil box, candles, and flint, prepared to make a day of it. Upon entering the church, she climbed the tower stairs to the chamber above the porch. The heavy oak door stood ajar, and she peeked in. Mr. Cushing saw her at once. He smiled broadly and waved her inside.

"My dear Miss Fairbanks!" he said. "What a discovery!"

Hannah smiled and took a chair. The little man was positively exuberant.

"Since I read his lordship's note this morning, I have been beside myself with anticipation. Anxious as a schoolboy! You must tell me everything," he said, bouncing slightly on his chair. "I have done no more than peer through the opening. Tell me what is down there."

She sat with him for a quarter hour and spoke about what she'd found, about her suspicions of an even older structure, about the reliquary. He was most enthusiastic about the latter. A saint's relic gave more importance to a church. The bishop would surely take notice.

Hannah explained her plans for the day and asked if there was a ladder or rope available to help her get in and out of the crypt.

"There is quite a good ladder in the barn off the rectory," he said, and then rose from his chair. "I shall go fetch it for you directly."

"Let me come with you and help carry it," Hannah said. She did not like to think of this small, elderly gentleman hauling a large ladder such a distance.

"No need, Miss Fairbanks," he said. "I shall ask Willie for assistance. He helps out at the rectory with his mother several days each week. He was pitching hay in the barn as I passed by this morning. You go on to the chancel and wait for us there."

Hannah followed him down the tower stairs. He turned around when he reached the porch and positively beamed. "I cannot tell you how thrilled I am, Miss Fairbanks. A Saxon crypt *and* a reliquary! It is all so exciting!" He gave a little chirp of pleasure, then bounded down the porch steps and toward the rectory, where he lived.

Mr. Cushing's excitement refueled her own. All thoughts of the earl and her foolish passion for him were left behind in the wake of tombs, effigies, reliquaries, and Roman cellars. Exhilaration mounted as she approached the chancel arch.

"I never meant for it to happen. I never thought to fall in love again."

Hannah stopped cold in her tracks. It was the earl's voice, coming from the direction of the Lady Chapel. A shudder skittered down her spine. To whom was he speaking?

"You will never be replaced in my heart, Amelia. Never. I hope you will understand."

Amelia. That had been the name of his first wife. Hannah remembered all the Prescott family tombs in the Lady Chapel. She had even made note of the late countess's pristine marble sepulcher.

Good heavens, he was speaking to his dead wife.

It embarrassed her to listen. It was too private, too intimate. And yet she stood bolted to floor, still as a stork, eavesdropping on words she had no right to hear. A sick feeling swelled inside her stomach like bread dough.

"I do not know what has taken me so long to recognize how perfect she is. She is beautiful and intelligent and kindhearted. And—forgive me, my love—extraordinarily desirable. She is everything I want in a wife. I plan to ask her to marry me tonight."

Oh, God. Oh, God. Oh, God. It was too soon. He was going to offer for Charlotte tonight. Tonight.

Her heart sank like a wounded bird.

He was going to marry Charlotte. Only one day after kissing Hannah so that her toes had practically curled up inside her half boots, he was going to propose to her sister. Hannah's stomach tied itself into knots, and she thought she might be sick. Her mouth became dry, and she could not seem to breathe.

She did not wish to hear anything more. She had to get out of here.

Her nerves were strung so tight she could hardly move. She very slowly and stiffly turned and began to walk back down the nave. She would not think of him. She would concentrate on putting one foot in front of the other. One step. One more step. Another step. Out of the church. Faster. Faster. Away.

She picked up her skirts and ran through the village, past the green, past the smithy, past the row of thatched cottages that lined the lane. Heedless of who might see her and what they might think, heedless of the stitch in her side, she ran and ran.

She ran across the Palladian bridge. She ran through the gatehouse and down the gravel path. Bypassing the main entrance, she ran to the west wing. When she opened the door of the western entry, she ran flat into the solid, broad chest of Major Prescott.

"Hold on there, Hannah girl," he said catching her by the elbows. "What's the rush so early in the morning? Don't tell me you've made another discovery?"

She gasped, panting for breath, unable to speak. The major kept his hold on her.

"Slowly now," he said. "Catch your breath. That's it. Take your time."

She took in great gulps of air through her mouth. A sharp pain in her side made it difficult to breathe. She bent slightly at the waist and would have fallen to her knees if the major hadn't held on.

After a few moments, she felt better and breathed more normally. "I need your help, Major," she said at last, still somewhat breathless.

"Anything, Hannah girl. I feel bad about leaving you stranded in that hole yesterday. What can I do to make up for it?"

"Will you take me to my brother's home in Lincolnshire?"

He drew back and shot her a puzzled look. "Your brother's home? Whatever for?"

"It is much too complicated to explain," she said. "But I need to leave right away. Now, in fact."

"Now?"

"Yes. It is quite urgent that I leave today as soon as possible. Will you take me? It is only a few hours' drive north, I believe."

The major furrowed his brows and stroked his chin. "I don't know, Hannah."

"Please, Major?" her voice sounded childishly plaintive, but she could not help it. "Please?"

"A few hours' north, you say?"

"Yes. Bertram—that's my brother, Sir Bertram Fairbanks—lives at Levering Park in Lincolnshire. It is near Great Baston, I believe."

He gave her a baleful look. What would she do if he refused? "All right," he said. "I suppose it is the least I can do after bungling your rescue yesterday."

Hannah almost collapsed with relief.

"But only on one condition," he said.

Oh, no. Please don't make this any more difficult, she thought.

"You had better tell me what's going on," he said. "I think I should know what I'm helping you run away from."

"All right," she said hesitantly. "I will explain everything. But not at this moment. I need to get my things together. I will tell you during the drive."

"I presume you are planning to bring along your maid?"

Hannah winced. She hadn't thought of that. "Oh, no," she said. "I couldn't. Lily is really Charlotte's maid. Besides, I do not want to make a public fuss. I just want to leave."

Major Prescott shook his head and clicked his tongue. "If you mean to travel two hours alone with me, then it will have to be in an open carriage. You had better dress warmly, my girl."

"I will."

"I wouldn't dare take Miles's curricle. He is still angry with me. There is an older curricle, from before my army days. Not quite so dashing, and I have no idea what condition it is in. I suppose we should take the barouche. I'll go round up the coachman."

"Oh, no, please. I'd rather not bother with a coachman." The fewer people involved in her escape, the better. Why had she not considered all these details before now? "Can we not take the older curricle?"

He stared at her quizzically. "I really cannot wait to hear your explanation for this sudden departure, Hannah. It must be quite a tale if you mean to make such a secret out of it. No maid. No coachman. This had better be good."

After arranging to meet him at the carriage barn in half an hour, Hannah dashed up the stairs to her bedchamber. She pulled a small portmanteau from her wardrobe and began to grab random articles of clothing and toss them inside. She would send for the rest of her things later.

Should she say anything to Charlotte—just to let her know she was leaving? No, that would not be wise. Charlotte would probably forbid it in any case. She would not wish another scene from Hannah. Besides, she would know that Bertram would not like it.

But, of course, Hannah would not be able to tell her sister the real reason for her departure. What could she say, anyway?

The earl is going to ask you to marry him tonight, and I cannot bear it. I'm in love with him myself, and it breaks my heart to think of him married to you.

Even if she had the nerve to say such a thing, how hateful it would sound. Hannah loved her sister. She really did. But not as Lord Strickland's wife. She was all wrong for him. Charlotte was vain and flighty and self-absorbed. She would make him miserable.

Charlotte would not be happy, either. Hannah could not imagine her sister settling into a quiet life in the country, regardless of how grand the estate was. Yet that was the sort of life Lord Strickland loved. His sheep, his farms, his tenants were all important to him.

And his daughters. What sort of mother would Charlotte make for them? She had never once expressed regret that her first marriage had been childless. Hannah had always suspected her sister was secretly relieved at having been denied motherhood. She was not fond of children.

How could Lord Strickland turn his daughters over to a woman who was not fond of children?

She slammed the portmanteau shut and fastened the lock. It was no use anguishing over something she could not change. Charlotte would get her offer tonight, and she would marry the earl. Hannah could not stop it from happening, even if she had the right to do so. Loving the earl did not give her that right.

But Hannah could not simply disappear without a word to her sister. Charlotte had been so solicitous the evening before, so concerned over Hannah's fall. When it became clear that Hannah was unharmed, Charlotte had sat and listened to her yammer on about the crypt, and had even gone so far as to pretend a measure of excitement on Hannah's behalf.

No matter what she thought of the unsuitability of a match with the earl, how could Hannah betray the sister who loved her?

She could not. She would keep her mouth shut for once, keep her opinions to herself. She would establish a life away from Charlotte and her new husband. She would throw herself into her studies and try to mend her own broken heart.

And she would never, never tell anyone the earl had kissed her.

For now, she must at least leave a note. Though she could not face Charlotte directly, she would write to her about her plans to visit Bertram. That way, at least, Charlotte would not have to worry.

Hannah sat down at the small writing desk and pulled out a sheet of parchment. She stared at it for long moments, not knowing what to write. But she could not afford the time to compose a perfect narrative. Without further thought, she scribbled a few lines, enough to explain her whereabouts.

She wished she had already written Bertram as she had meant to do. Why had she not done so? She had put it off until it was too late. She would simply have to arrive unannounced and hope his wife, Martha, would take her in.

Hannah folded the note and walked across the corridor to Charlotte's bedchamber. Fortunately, her sister had got into the habit of country hours and, at least while at Epping Hall, no longer slept until noon. She would be downstairs at breakfast, or strolling through the gardens with Cousin Winifred. Or so Hannah hoped.

Listening at the door to ensure the room was empty, she crept inside. She left the note on the dressing table, propped next to a porcelain scent bottle, where Charlotte was certain to see it.

Hannah returned to her room and tugged on a bonnet and a heavy wool pelisse. She grabbed her portmanteau, headed down the service stairs, and on with the rest of her life.

Chapter 17

"Good heavens, Charlotte! What is it?"

She had walked into Miles's study and stood before his desk, looking as though she might collapse. He rushed to her side and guided her to a chair. All color had drained from her face, but for some reason he could not explain, she looked neither frightened nor ill. She looked angry.

Good Lord. Had Hannah said something? Had she told Charlotte how he'd kissed her?

He stifled a groan and composed himself, thinking how best to handle the situation. Of course, he planned to marry Hannah, so there should be no concern that she had been compromised. Charlotte would be angry on her own behalf. She may feel that Miles had led her to believe in the eventuality of her own betrothal to him.

Of course, he had done no such thing. It had been everyone else who had set those expectations. Damn them all.

He took a deep breath and leaned back against his desk. "Please, Charlotte. Tell me what has happened."

She pressed her fingers to her temple and grimaced as though in some kind of pain. "I cannot believe it," she said. "I simply cannot believe it."

Oh, dear. This was going to be difficult. He gave her a questioning look, allowing her to take the lead in this discussion. He had no wish to admit to anything until he understood how much she knew.

She heaved a deep sigh that verged on a moan. "Hannah has eloped with your brother."

Miles almost lost his balance and slid to the floor. He had been braced for something else entirely. "I beg your pardon," he said incredulously. He must have heard wrong.

"I said Hannah, my baby sister, has eloped with Major Prescott."

"I don't believe it."

"Well then, perhaps you should read this." She handed him a folded piece of parchment.

A sudden vague foreboding engulfed him. He took the letter carefully between his fingers as though it might burn him. He opened it and glanced at Hannah's scrawled name at the bottom of the page. Good God, what had she done?

Lottie,

I have gone north with Major Prescott. You will know my destination. You will understand it is not an ideal situation, though perhaps I may find some contentment with him. It seems the best solution since you will soon be married. Please do not worry.

Yours,
Hannah

Miles stared at the note in disbelief. "But this is madness," he said.

"My thoughts exactly," Charlotte said. "I know Hannah can be impulsive at times, but I had thought better of your brother. What are we going to do?"

It made no sense. He was sure George was going to make Rachel an offer. At least he had assumed their renewed courtship was progressing in that direction. Had he missed something? Had it all gone sour and he'd been too wrapped up in his confusion over Hannah and Charlotte to notice?

Hannah! What had he done to her?

There was no question in his mind that it was all his own fault. All because he'd kissed Hannah. She was running away from that kiss. He had unlocked her sensuality, and it had confused her. Probably frightened her. More important, she still believed he was going to marry Charlotte. Poor Hannah no doubt felt that she had betrayed her sister with her response to that kiss. And so she had decided to do the one thing that would eliminate any hint of disloyalty or betrayal. She would marry someone else. Against all her previous convictions to the contrary, she would marry.

And somehow George had been willing to cooperate. Damn him! Had all that flirting with Hannah been serious after all? Had Rachel rejected him, and so he had rebounded with Hannah?

"I swear I'll kill him," Miles said aloud.

"Preferably before they reach Gretna Green," Charlotte said. "Are you going after them?"

"Of course I am."

Miles darted into the hallway outside his study and grabbed the first footman he saw. He sent a message to the stables to have his curricle brought round, and another to have his greatcoat, hat, and gloves sent down.

"I'm going with you." He turned to find Charlotte standing behind him.

"She's my sister and my responsibility." She looked chagrined. "I fear I am in large part to blame for this. I have scolded and chastised and corrected the girl until she could not take any more. I ought to have left her alone with her books and her architecture. I had no right to try to change her into something else."

"You are too hard on yourself," Miles said. "I don't imagine you are to blame at all." It was his fault, he thought, not hers.

She smiled. "You are very kind to say so, but I still blame myself. Just the same, I have every intention of boxing the girl's ears when I next see her. Besides, you cannot bring her back alone. You will need me for propriety's sake."

She was right about that, though he wondered if this was a clever maneuver on her part to be alone with him in a carriage. He would set her straight on that point at once.

"Yes, of course you must come," he said. "Since I am taking my curricle to make the best time, you need not worry about your own reputation. An open carriage should provide no hint of impropriety."

She gave a coy smile as if he had indeed bested her. He would perhaps tell her the full truth while on the road.

A maid was summoned to bring Charlotte's bonnet and a heavy cloak. By the time the curricle was wheeled into the drive, they were ready to go.

He lifted Charlotte up onto the seat and was about to climb up himself when a shout from the entry stopped him.

"What's all the commotion? Where the devil is everyone going in such a hurry?" Joseph stood on the steps of the Tudor porch with Rachel by his side.

Miles groaned. Could this get any more complicated?

If he hadn't known Miles better, Joseph would think the two of them were running off together. Something cagey was going on, he'd be bound. Miles walked toward him, his face pinched with agitation.

"I say, Miles, you look like you've been caught with your fingers in the honey pot. What's going on, old boy?"

Miles darted several glances in Rachel's direction.

"Something's come up," he said enigmatically. "Charlotte and I will be gone for a while."

Joseph gave him a wicked grin and slapped him on the shoulder. "You dog!" he said, then lowered his voice. "Are you whisking away the lovely widow for a bit of . . . sport?"

"No!" Miles did not look in the least amused. He glanced at Rachel again. "Look, I'm sorry, but something's happened. You are bound to find out sooner or later." He looked straight at Rachel when he continued. "It seems Hannah and George have run off together. Eloped."

"What?" Joseph turned to Rachel and watched the blood drain from her face. He grabbed her hand. "It's not possible."

"So I would have thought," Miles said. "But Hannah left a note. There is no question. They are headed north, no doubt to Gretna Green. I'm so sorry, Rachel. I had thought . . ."

"I don't believe it." Joseph did not for one minute believe that George Prescott had eloped with Hannah Fairbanks. Only last night George had asked his permission to make Rachel an offer. Such a formality was not necessary since Rachel was of age and they'd all known each other for years. But it had been a gesture Joseph had appreciated. George had said he had not spoken to Rachel yet. He had planned to do so this evening after supper.

If he had gone haring off with Hannah, it was not to marry her. Joseph would stake his life on it.

"Listen, Miles," he said, "this is a sticky situation. Perhaps it would be best if I went with you instead of Lady Abingdon."

"She insists on going," Miles replied. "And there's no time to argue about it now. I have to go." He walked back toward the curricle.

"I really think you should take me along," Joseph

said. He needed to tell Miles the truth, but not in front of Rachel, or Lady Abingdon.

"I'm sorry, Joe, there's no room for you up here," Miles said as he swung himself up onto the seat.

"Miles, it is very important that I be there when you find them." Miles gave him a look that implied he understood, though of course he did not.

"If you want to beat George to a pulp," Miles said as he flicked the reins, "you will have to wait until after I have wrung his foolish neck. If you insist on coming, you had better follow in another carriage. I do not have time to wait." With that, he guided the horses around the courtyard and out the entrance.

Joseph looked down at Rachel. She appeared to be on the verge of tears. He squeezed her hand. "Don't you worry, Rachel. It is not what you think."

"How can it not be?" she said, her voice choking on a sob. "He has run off with Hannah. He has betrayed me again."

"No, I do not think so."

"I should have seen it coming," she continued. "He's been flirting with her like mad ever since his return. I should have known he hadn't changed."

"Rachel." He let go of her hand and put his arm around her shoulder. "Listen to me." He tilted her face up with his other hand. "Listen to me."

If he hadn't spoken to George the night before, the look on Rachel's face would have broken his heart. "George has not run off with Hannah," he said.

"How do you know?"

"Because he loves you."

Tears trembled on her lashes and then rolled down her cheeks. "I thought he did," she said in a quavering voice. "But he's made a fool of me again."

"No, he hasn't. I'll prove it to you."

Her brow furrowed in puzzlement. "How?"

"You and I are going to follow Miles and Lady

Abingdon. When we catch up with George and Hannah, I think you will find that something else entirely is going on. And it has nothing to do with George. Or you."

"I don't understand."

"I cannot say anything more," Joseph said. "But I tell you, George has not run away with Hannah. Whatever has happened, I will wager it has more to do with Miles than with George."

"Miles?"

"Let me see if there are any carriages left, and I'll explain on the way."

While Rachel went to put on a coat and bonnet, Joseph walked to the carriage barn to see for himself what sort of vehicle was available.

He found that George had also taken a curricle, so there were no other fast sporting carriages available. If Miles had taken the time to learn the miscreants had taken a curricle, he would have known they had not planned to travel all the way to Scotland.

There was Miles's chariot, however, a small, well-sprung traveling carriage that should make good speed. Joseph had it made ready and sent for the coachman.

A quarter hour later, the chariot was brought round to the courtyard entrance. When he and Rachel were about to climb inside, Winifred stepped out onto the porch. "Hello there. Are you going home?"

Joseph grinned and shook his head. "Nothing so simple as that," he said. "We are about to chase after Miles and Lady Abingdon, who are chasing after George and Hannah."

Winifred cocked her head to one side and furrowed her brow. "Why on earth would you all want to go to Levering Park?"

Joseph pulled Rachel to his side. He suspected

Winifred knew something that would put her mind at ease. "I beg your pardon, Winifred. Levering Park?"

"Is that not where you're going?"

Joseph laughed. "I have no idea where we're going. We're simply following Miles, who is, as I said, following George."

"Well, that's where George was going."

Joseph looked down at Rachel and winked. "So George and Hannah are not on their way to Gretna Green?"

Winifred stared at them dumbly for a moment, then burst into laughter. "Is that what everyone thinks? Oh, my goodness. Well, of course George is not eloping with Hannah. He is taking Hannah to her brother's estate in Lincolnshire. Sir Bertram Fairbanks lives at Levering Park. George agreed to drive Hannah there. Since Bertram is Godfrey's cousin, George thought we might have directions to the place. As it happens, we have visited there once or twice. I wrote down the directions for George and off he went. Eloped?" She laughed again and reached out to touch Rachel's arm. "No, my dear, he has not eloped with Hannah. Do you not know that he only has eyes for you?"

"You see?" Joseph said. "What did I tell you. Nothing at all to worry about. Oh, but I say, we'd better get to Miles before he murders the lad."

"And so he will," Winifred said, "if he thinks George has stolen Hannah."

"Aha!" Joseph exclaimed. "So you've noticed it, too?"

"Yes, and I believe he has finally noticed it for himself. Strange, is it not? I was so sure he'd fall in love with Charlotte. Now, be off with you. I shall give the coachman directions to Levering Park. It is a lovely place, less than two hours north, I'd say. I am sure you will find George and Hannah there."

Winifred stood on the porch and waved to them as

the chariot was swung around the courtyard and out the entrance.

Levering Park was indeed a lovely place, Winifred thought. It had been years since she'd been there. The grounds were full of deer and there was a lovely little stream, as she recalled, stocked with trout. The twins would enjoy such a place.

She must run her husband to ground and convince him of the advantages of a drive to Levering Park. Surely, he could have no objection to visiting his own cousin. He did not enjoy being closed up in a carriage with the twins for long at a time, so perhaps he would choose to ride. But, by Jove, she would insist that they go. Otherwise, they would be all alone at Epping, since everyone else was chasing after one another.

Besides, the day could turn out to be most interesting, and she did not want to miss any of the excitement.

Chapter 18

"I do not understand this at all," Miles said as he leaped back upon the seat of his curricle. "The ostler said they did not take the Leicester Road, but went on toward Stamford."

They had stopped at inn after inn following the trail of George and Hannah. They discovered George had taken the old curricle, the one he used to drive before he'd joined the army. The ostlers at almost every inn remembered its chipped paint and split leather hood, wondering why two fine bits of blood were pulling such a battered vehicle. The gentlemen at the ribbons was certainly not going to impress his young lady with that old pile of sticks, one of them had joked.

The odd thing was, the trail had not gone in the direction Miles had expected. They would need to head west before meeting up with the Great North Road, the quickest route to Gretna Green.

"Could they be trying to put us off the scent, do you think?" Charlotte asked. "Going north when they know we would expect them to go west?"

"I don't know why they should go into Lincolnshire," Miles replied. "I confess I am thoroughly puzzled."

"I have a brother in Lincolnshire," Charlotte said. "But I don't suppose that has any bearing on the matter."

"It is all very strange," Miles said. "And why

wouldn't they have taken a traveling carriage instead of that beat-up old curricle? Or hired a chaise if they wanted to be anonymous? I begin to wonder if we have mistaken the whole matter."

"But Hannah's letter . . ."

"Yes, the letter." He flicked the reins and steered the team out of the inn yard at Gretton and onto the road toward Stamford. "About that letter."

"Yes?"

Miles squirmed a bit on the seat. This was most awkward, but it had to be said. "In her letter, Hannah mentioned that you were to be married soon." He took a long breath. "I presume she believed you would be married to me."

Charlotte gave an elegant shrug. "I have no idea what she meant, I am sure."

"Charlotte, this is difficult for me, but I need to make matters clear between us before we run my brother and Hannah to earth."

"Yes?"

Oh Lord. Her studied indifference only made her sound more expectant. "I wish to apologize if I have allowed you to misunderstand my feelings for you, if I have encouraged any false expectations."

She stiffened slightly on the bench. "I'm sure I do not know what you mean."

"Charlotte." Why couldn't she be as forthright as her sister? Why did she have to play these games? "From the moment you arrived at Epping, everyone—most especially my interfering sister—seemed to have decided that I should marry you. You are a very beautiful and charming woman, Charlotte. You were even tempting enough to kiss that one time. But I confess, I do not wish to marry you."

She was silent for a long moment, then heaved a resigned sigh. "Well," she said. "That certainly clears matters up, does it not?"

"I'm sorry, Charlotte. It's a beastly thing to have to say to a woman. But I thought it best to have it out in the open."

She gave a mirthless chuckle. "I appreciate your candor, my lord. But I assure you, I was under no such misapprehension."

"Honestly?" He did not believe her.

"Honestly. Please do not feel you are under any obligation to explain yourself to me."

"But I would like to, if you'll allow me."

He glanced over to her and she nodded. He returned his attention to the team and took a steadying breath. "You see, there is someone else."

"Oh?" Only a tiny shift in her position indicated her surprise. He wished he could see her face. Or perhaps not. Looking at her would only make him more uncomfortable.

"I confess, it has taken me quite off guard. I never expected anything like this to happen to me again. But the truth is . . . the truth is I have fallen in love with your sister."

Charlotte sat bolt upright on the bench and twisted her body around to face him. "With Hannah?"

Miles almost laughed at the shock in her voice. "Believe me, Charlotte, it surprises me as much as it does you. But there you have it. I love her. And if we catch up with her before she makes the mistake of marrying my brother—who is, by the way, in love with Rachel Wetherby—then I plan to ask Hannah to marry me."

"Hannah?" He felt her shrink beside him on the bench. "Hannah?"

"I'm sorry if I've shocked you. It was not at all what I intended, I assure you. It just . . . happened."

"Is that why she ran away?"

"Probably. I think she knew of my interest in her. Of my carnal interest, anyway. I kissed her, you see. I believe she must have felt she'd betrayed you by allowing me to kiss her."

"Well, then. Well." Charlotte's hands fidgeted in her lap, and she fell silent.

Miles did not know what else to say. He'd probably said too much already. Hannah's influence, he supposed. He smiled to think what other changes in his character she would affect.

After a few moments, he sensed Charlotte's shoulders had begun to shake. Good Lord, she was crying. He had not been prepared for that. Anger, yes. But tears?

"Charlotte, I'm sorry—"

His words were cut short by her laughter. Laughter, not tears!

"No, my lord, it is I who am sorry." She continued to chuckle softly. "It is all so absurd, I cannot help but laugh. Here I was trying to change Hannah into a pattern card of a proper lady so she could go to London and find a husband. I despaired of her ever taking, you know. And look what has happened?" She laughed aloud. "She won the biggest prize of them all without any help from me. What an arrogant shrew I have been! It is no wonder you fell in love with her and not with me."

Her laughter sent waves of relief washing over him. He had been so afraid he'd hurt her, misled her. Perhaps he had. Yet here she was being so philosophical about it, he wanted to reach over and kiss her.

"Charlotte, I cannot tell you how relieved I am that you are taking this so well. I feared I might have caused you pain."

"Oh, my pride is wounded, to be sure," she said. "I always thought myself so . . . so attractive to men. It is well to puncture my ego now and then. And to have my clumsy little sister steal a beat on me is good for my character."

"You are a marvelous woman, Charlotte," Miles said. "If Hannah and George have already tied the knot before we find them, I believe I shall ask you to marry me after all."

"Oh, please don't," she said with a laugh. "I would always know I was second best, and that would never do. Besides, it is just as well that I should not marry you, for I find I am not at all suited to a bucolic life in the country. I hope you will not take offense, my lord, but I am sure I would be bored silly within a fortnight. All those sheep!"

Just when Hannah figured matters could not get any worse, an axle had split on the curricle, sending them into a ditch. She ought to have known she could not get through even one day without a major bungle of some sort. She could not seem to keep a dress clean to save her life. She seemed destined to find herself sprawled on floors, stumbling into holes, or falling into ditches. It was only to be expected—probably related to some star or other she'd been born under.

She and Major Prescott walked the mile or so to the village of Great Baston, leading the horses but abandoning the curricle wreckage in the ditch. When she had expressed concern about going on to Levering Park, he promised to hire a chaise at the first suitable inn.

He had procured a private parlor for her at The Swan, the only inn in Great Baston. She enjoyed a restorative cup of tea while the major saw about hiring a chaise. Hannah had told him everything. Since he, too, believed the earl was going to marry Charlotte, he was very understanding about her need to get away. He would help her get to Bertram's, no matter what it took.

There was a bit of commotion in the yard below when another carriage pulled in. Hannah could hear sounds of shouting and talking, but paid little mind. She needed the time to consider her future. The immediate future loomed particularly heavy. How was she to explain to Bertram her sudden appearance on his doorstep?

As she pondered various excuses she might make to Bertram and Martha for intruding on their home, she heard footsteps on the stairs. Major Prescott must have completed his arrangements. Hannah set out another cup, thinking he might want a bit of tea before going on. She was pouring the tea when the parlor door opened.

"Hannah."

The familiar voice caused her hand to jerk, sloshing tea across the table and onto her skirt. Oh God. What was he doing here?

She heard him walk into the room, but she did not look up. She did not want to see him. Her dress was stained with mud, and now tea, and he probably stood there as clean and shiny as a brass farthing. She did not want to see him.

"Hannah." He was right beside her. "Why did you run away?" Oh, that voice. It was not his formal voice. It was the one he'd used when he'd held her at the ball, and before he'd kissed her at St. Biddulph's. It threatened to disarm her.

"I had to," she said.

"Would you turn around and look at me, Hannah?"

"No."

"Why not?"

"I don't want to. I don't want to look at you."

He touched her lightly on the shoulder and she flinched. "But I need you to look at me," he said. "I need to see your eyes. I want to tell you something, and I need to see you. Please, Hannah. Please turn around."

She was no match for that voice. Or his touch. Why was he doing this to her?

She turned around in her chair and looked up at him. He smiled and took both her hands and pulled her to her feet. He did not let go.

"When I kissed you yesterday, you were too upset to listen to me," he said. "You would not let me answer all your questions. Will you listen to me now?"

She nodded her head, steeling herself for more apologies and confessions about Charlotte. She dropped her gaze, unable to meet his eyes.

"First, I want you to know that I am not going to marry Charlotte. I've already told her so."

Her head jerked up. "You told Lottie you don't want to marry her?"

"Yes."

"Merciful heavens! What did she do?"

He smiled and squeezed her hands. "She was wonderful. Very understanding. Especially when I told her there was someone else."

"There is?" her heart began to beat wildly, and Hannah tried to quell the twinge of hope that fluttered in her breast. He pulled her closer.

"Yes. It's you, Hannah. You're the one I want to marry."

"Me?" Her voice came out in a squeak.

"You."

"But . . . but I heard you this morning," she stammered, trying to make sense of what he said. "I heard you in the church talking to . . . to Amelia. You said you were going to ask Charlotte to marry you tonight."

"Not Charlotte. You."

"You were talking about *me*?"

"Yes," he said, smiling down at her with those luscious brown eyes. He laughed at the expression of stark incredulity she did not even try to disguise.

"And now I think I understand why you bolted. You must have run away before you heard everything."

"I ran like the very devil."

He laughed again and pulled her tight against his chest. "That is a shame," he said. "If you had stayed longer, you would have heard me say how much I love you."

"You do?"

"With all my heart," he said, then kissed the corners of her mouth. "I confess it took me a while to figure it out. You blasted away all my best intentions. I was never going to fall in love again. I certainly never expected it. Never even hoped for it. Yet here I am, wildly in love with you, loving everything about you."

"Oh, my goodness!"

"I love how you can't seem to keep your hair pinned up and how your curls are always tumbling down. I love how this dimple begins to twitch when you are trying not to laugh. I love the way your blue eyes flash with uninhibited enthusiasm when you talk about Saxon arches and Norman transepts. I love all your little mishaps and the way you always seem to be tripping over your own feet. I love the sound of your laughter. Shall I go on?"

"Oh, my lord!"

He laughed and kissed her nose. "Assuming you are addressing me and not the Almighty, I suggest it is high time you called me Miles."

She could not believe this was happening. It was not a dream. It was real. He loved her! She wrapped her arms around his neck and tried out his name. "Miles."

"Hannah."

He kissed her then, on the mouth, gently at first. So soft, so tender it made her feel like weeping. She moaned against his lips, and he pulled her tighter. Suddenly, his kiss became more urgent, nibbling, tasting, biting, as though he wanted to devour her. When

Hannah gave a small sigh of sheer pleasure, his tongue traced the edge of her lips, compelling them to part. Her body melted against his as he plunged his tongue into her mouth.

Hannah thought she might die from the pure sensation of it all, the way his tongue caressed her own, drawing her deeper, deeper into his mouth. And then he was trailing kisses over her jaw and down her neck and around her ear, and back again to ravish her mouth.

When he finally pulled away, they were both panting and breathless. He rested his forehead against hers. "I love you, Hannah."

"I think I have loved you since the very first day," she said. "I was so jealous of Lottie when I thought you wanted her. Why would you want a clumsy, unsophisticated girl like me?"

He kissed her lightly on the mouth. "I'll tell you why. You strip me of everything false and unimportant. You free me. You liberate me. You make me want to fly. You make me want to soar up into your dazzling light."

She laughed. "My what?"

"Your light," he said. "You are full of life and light. You are radiant with it. I want you to set me free to bask in it."

"Miles. I don't understand you. But I do love you."

"Will you marry me, then?"

Oh, my. Oh, my. Her head was spinning. He really and truly wanted to marry her. But she would be tied to more than just Miles. He had a family. "What about Amy and Caro?" she asked. "How will they feel about it?"

"They love you," he said. "And I've already told Amy. She is very pleased. Can I tell her you said yes?"

Hannah hesitated only for the merest instant, then only because it was still so difficult to believe it was real. But she would not give him time to change his mind. "Yes!" She rained kisses all across his face. "Yes, yes, yes!"

He laughed beneath her kisses. "Even though you never wanted to be married?"

"That was only because I thought early church architecture was more interesting," she said, still kissing him. "Of course, that was before I met you. Besides, if I marry you, I can still keep up my studies. I can spend all my days at St. Biddulph's."

"And all your nights with me."

Hannah blushed at his words, but only because they excited her. He laughed at her discomposure and kissed her.

They were interrupted by a knock at the door. "Is everything settled in there?"

Miles put Hannah away from him and straightened his crushed cravat. "Yes, George. You may come in." He whispered to Hannah, "I was ready to murder him, you know. We thought the two of you had eloped."

"What?"

George and Charlotte entered the parlor, followed by Joseph and Rachel.

"Ah," Miles said, "I see we are joined by two more. Joe, I trust you have discovered it is not necessary to throttle my brother?"

"Good heavens!" Hannah said. "What are you all doing here?"

"It seems there was a dearth of white knights to rescue you yesterday, Hannah girl," the major said. "And so when it looked as though you needed rescuing again today, the whole regiment was sent in."

Hannah had no idea what he was talking about. "Consider me well rescued," she said, moving to stand close to Miles, desperately wanting to touch him, but a little wary of how he would feel about her doing so in public.

"Well, brother," the major said, grinning at Miles, "is there something you'd like to tell us?"

"Indeed there is," Miles said. He took Hannah's hand and placed it decorously upon his arm. She suspected it was as much of a public display of affection she was ever likely to receive from him. That was fine with her, so long as he fulfilled the promise of those nights he mentioned.

"I am pleased to report," he continued, "that Miss Hannah Fairbanks has agreed to be my wife."

The major and Mr. Wetherby each sent up a cheer. Rachel Wetherby offered quieter congratulations. Hannah looked at her sister, uncertain what to expect. But when Charlotte opened her arms, Hannah flew into them.

"You have stolen a march on me, little one," Charlotte said. "But I shall not hold it against you. You deserve his love. I am sorry I tried so hard to change things. I meant well, Hannah. I just got it all wrong. The important thing is for you to be happy."

"Oh, Lottie, I am bursting with happiness." She hugged her sister tight. "I am sorry, though, that you were never able to make a lady out of me."

"But my dear girl," Charlotte said, "you do not need to be a lady. You are going to be a countess!"

Everyone laughed until the major held up a hand for silence. "Miles, old man," he said, "you were slow enough settling matters with Hannah that I had time to do a bit of settling of my own. I am proud to say that Rachel has agreed to marry me."

Another round of back-slapping and congratulations followed the major's announcement.

"Good heavens!" Charlotte exclaimed. "I suppose that means I shall have to set my cap for you, Mr. Wetherby, since all the other gentlemen are taken."

Joseph's expression was one of such terror they all began to laugh.

*   *   *

It was decided that since they were so close to Levering Park, the entire group should pay Sir Bertram Fairbanks a visit. Miles thought it only proper to call upon his future brother-in-law, though he would rather have been expected. Charlotte, however, was adamant that her brother would welcome them.

Miles rode in the curricle with Hannah at his side. The other four were crammed into the chariot. Miles let the chariot lead the way, allowing him a small measure of privacy with Hannah. They kissed and touched as much as possible without Miles losing control of the team. He could not seem to keep his hands off her. When they reached the gates of Levering Park, Miles had to help Hannah pin up her hair and straighten her dress. His own cravat was a lost cause. Perhaps Sir Bertram, who did not know him, would think it a deliberately casual style.

As the two vehicles rolled up the drive, Miles noticed another large carriage had just arrived. He would swear it was one of Godfrey's.

When they came to a stop, he watched as four children bounded from the other carriage. By Jove, it was his own daughters and the twins, followed by Win and Godfrey. What the devil were they doing here?

He stepped out of the chariot and quickly handed Hannah down before he was accosted by a daughter on each leg. Amy bounced with excitement.

"Did you ask her? Did you ask her?"

He scooped Amy up into his arms. Hannah picked up Caro and nuzzled her nose. "Yes, I asked her," he said.

"Well, what did she say?"

"I said yes," Hannah replied for him.

The two little girls clapped their hands and cheered. Caro kissed Hannah. Amy reached over to kiss her, too. Miles almost kissed her as well, but remembered himself in time.

Once Winifred had fussed and cried over both her brothers and their betrothals, she took charge of gathering up the entire group and herding them to the entrance of Levering Park. Eight adults and four children were paraded through the entrance while Sir Bertram and Lady Fairbanks stood beside the doorway and gaped in astonishment as the crowd of uninvited guests streamed into their home.

Miles, Hannah, and the girls kept up the rear. There seemed to be an unspoken agreement to huddle together and keep their private happiness to themselves for as long as possible. Miles considered the four of them, smiling and happy, and swallowed a lump in his throat. They were a family. Already, they were a family, all loving one another as if they'd always been together.

God willing, they would always be together. This was what he had wanted. This was what he had missed. It wasn't so much a question of replacing Amelia, whom he would always love in his heart. It was the need to be a family again—a whole family, complete with a mother, and perhaps even more children.

Though he had set out to arrange a simple, uncomplicated marriage with a mature woman, his heart had led him to a better place. To a miracle. To Hannah.